Acclaim for *I Got Somebody in Staunton*

"Lewis beautifully renders the odd, quiet moments before and after life's explosive events. . . . Lewis creates unique characters, individuals defined by much more than their race, whose complexity leads to surprising destinations."
— *Entertainment Weekly*

"Magnificent description brings to life characters we all have encountered, but Lewis has done it exactingly and with a minimum of words. That is the mark of an accomplished writer no matter what his genre." — *Richmond Times-Dispatch*

"There is greatness here, all over the place, plain and simple. Sentence by sentence, this deeply felt and lyrical collection proves that Lewis is a master of the short story. *I Got Somebody in Staunton* has more warmth than almost any recent book I can remember; I'd urge it on anyone."
— Dave Eggers,
author of *A Heartbreaking Work of Staggering Genius*

"William Henry Lewis is both an artistic and a political writer . . . [with] a notable gift for prose poetry."
— *Washington Post Book World*

"Haunting, nuanced short stories. With his effortless elegance, ease, and economy of language, Lewis stands as an important reminder that, in this hectic, sped-up world, the best things are still well worth waiting for." — *Elle*

"Lyrical, risk-taking collection. Lewis renders beautifully the sadness of both those left behind and those who've done the leaving." — *O* magazine

"Lewis crafts a thoughtful, appealing collection deeply concerned with the pride and pain of African American heritage. . . . The cumulative effect of these ten pieces is unquestionably powerful." — *Publishers Weekly*

I Got Somebody in Staunton

ALSO BY

WILLIAM HENRY LEWIS

In the Arms of Our Elders

Stories

I Got Somebody in Staunton

william henry lewis

Amistad

An Imprint of HarperCollinsPublishers

A hardcover edition of this book was published in 2005 by Amistad, an imprint of HarperCollins Publishers.

I GOT SOMEBODY IN STAUNTON.
Copyright © 2005, 2006 by William Henry Lewis.

Grateful acknowledgment is made to the following publications in which some of these stories first appeared: "In the Swamp," *African American Review;* "I Got Somebody in Staunton," *Callaloo;* "Urban Renewal," *Colorado Review;* "Potcake," *Kenyon Review;* "Kudzu," *Ploughshares;* "Rossonian Days," *New Letters;* "Shades," *Ploughshares.*

First Amistad paperback edition published 2006.

BOOK DESIGN AND TITLE PAGE PHOTOGRAPHY
DEBORAH KERNER / DANCING BEARS DESIGN

The Library of Congress has cataloged the hardcover edition as follows:

Lewis, William Henry
I got somebody in Staunton : stories / William Henry Lewis.—1st ed.
p. cm.
ISBN 0-06-053665-9 (alk. paper)
1. African Americans—Fiction. I. Title.

PS3562.E983I2 2005
813'.54—dc22   2004055128

ISBN-13: 978-0-06-053666-4 (pbk.)
ISBN-10: 0-06-053666-7

06 07 08 09 10 BVG/RRD 10 9 8 7 6 5 4 3 2 1

THIS BOOK IS FOR LESLYE,

WHOSE STORY WILL CONTINUE

THROUGH ME.

The whole thing, the story . . .

like music heard from far off.

SHERWOOD ANDERSON

• • •

People live before us leave a memory behind;

forming, moving in a circle,

Ghosts appearing through the sound

waving at us from the distance . . .

ABBEY LINCOLN

• • •

Acknowledgments

Ten years have passed between my first book and this one. Such a passage produces a long list of gratitude. The beauty of Virginia's land and people filled the early years of my passage in such a way that will never leave me. For three years after Virginia I made my home among the big-hearted people of Brooklyn. I will always have much love for Dean Street. I spent the last four of those ten years making my home in the Bahamas. I owe the blessing of that time to the College of the Bahamas, the Bahamas Football Association, and all the wonderful Bahamians who made me a part of their communities. Thanks especially to the Carey, Seymour, Roker, Bartlett, Stubbs, and Gongora families, and, of course, my family in Bears Football Club.

The words that make up this book could not have been made without the sharp eyes and honest wisdom of Fred Pfeil, Michelle Cliff, Deborah E. McDowell, Neil Arditi, Bliss Broyard, Maud Casey, Erica Gentry, Lauren McIntyre, Lisa Williams, Stephen Belber, Jeremy Norton, and Sue Houchins, the friend you hope every mentor will become. My quality of life as a writer who teaches owes much to George Garrett, one of the finest examples of how to live and love a life in words.

Many thanks to those journal editors who first published

many of these stories: *African American Review, Callaloo, Colorado Review, Kenyon Review New Letters*. Special thanks to Don Lee, at *Ploughshares,* and to Ann Beattie, whose editorial assistance helped form "Shades" into the well-traveled story it has become. I am also grateful for the editors of *Speak My Name, The Cry of an Occasion, The African American West: A Century of Short Stories, Gumbo*, and *What the Thunder Meant*, who chose my fiction for those wonderful anthologies.

I am honored that this book was made possible with support from the Virginia Commission for the Arts, and the Fellowship of Southern Writers. My deeply felt thanks go out as well to Marita Golden and the Zora Neale Hurston/Richard Wright Foundation, whose spirit has raised opportunities, and the bar, for all writers and readers. I also wish to recognize the generosity of the University of Missouri, Kansas City, and the brothers and sisters at Albany State University, for cherishing our artists in the old way.

There is a long list of friends to whom I am indebted for carrying me this far, but none has carried me so often or as soulfully as Nathanael Fareed Mahluli, friend who is my brother, and Jason Page, brother who is my friend. I live because you do.

No one would be reading this book without Nina Graybill; when other agents wanted novels, she believed in these stories and got this book where it needed to be. These words would not work as they do without my editors, Dawn Davis and Stacey Barney, whose vision saw me through the work and whose care saw the work through.

Finally, this book's author would not be here without my family, who are my breath, and Sarah, who has been a precious gift in my life.

Contents

Shades

I was fourteen that summer. August brought heat I had never known, and during the dreamlike drought of those days I saw my father for the first time in my life. The tulip poplars faded to yellow before September came. There had been no rain for weeks, and the people's faces along Eleventh Street wore a longing for something cool and wet, something distant, like the promise of a balmy October. Talk of weather was of the heat and the dry taste in their mouths. And they were frustrated, having to notice something other than the weather in their daily pleasantries. Sometimes, in the haven of afternoon porch shade or in the still and cooler places of late night, they drank and laughed, content because they had managed to make it through the day.

What I noticed was the way the skin of my neighbors glistened as they toiled in their backyards, trying to save their gardens or working a few more miles into their cars. My own skin surprised me each morning in the mirror, becoming darker and darker, my hair lightening, dispelling my assumption that it had always been a curly black—the whole of me a new and stranger blend of browns from day after day of basketball on asphalt courts or racing the other boys down the street after the Icee truck each afternoon.

I came to believe that it was the heat that made things happen. It was a summer of empty sidewalks, people I knew drifting through the alleyways where trees gave more shade, the dirt there cooler to walk on than any paved surface. Strangers would walk through the neighborhood seemingly lost, the dust and sun's glare making the place look like somewhere else they were trying to go. Sitting on our porch, I watched people I'd never seen before walk by and melt into those rippling pools of heat glistening above the asphalt as if something must be happening just beyond where that warmth quivered down the street. At night I'd look out from the porch of our house, a few blocks off Eleventh, and scan the neighborhood, wanting some change, something besides the nearby rumble of freight trains and the monotony of heat, something refreshing and new. In heat like that, everyone sat on their porches looking out into the night and hoping for something better to come up with the sun.

It was during such a summer, my mother told me, that my father got home from the third shift at the bottling plant, waked her with his naked body already on top of her, entered her before she was able to say no, sweated on her through moments of whiskey breath and indolent thrusting, came without saying a word, and walked back out of our house forever. He never uttered a word, she said, for it was not his way to speak much when it was hot. My mother was a wise woman and spoke almost as beautifully as she sang. She told me he left with the rumble of the trains. She told me this with a smooth, distant voice as if it were the story of someone else, and it was strange to me that she might have wanted to cry at something like that but didn't, as if there were no need anymore.

She said she lay still after he left, certain only of his sweat and the workshirt he left behind. She lay still for at least an hour, aware of two things: feeling the semen her body wouldn't hold slowly dripping onto the sheets, and knowing that some part of what her body did hold would fight and form itself into what became me, nine months later.

I was ten years old when she told me this. After she sat me down and said this is how you came to me, I knew that I would never feel like I was ten for the rest of that year. She told me what it was to love someone, what it was to make love to someone, and what it took to make someone. Sometimes, she told me, all three don't happen at once. I didn't quite know what that meant, but I felt her need to tell me. She seemed determined not to hold it from me. It seemed as if somehow she was pushing me ahead of my growing. And I felt uncomfortable with it, the way secondhand shoes are at first comfortless. I grew to know the discomfort as a way of living.

After that she filled my home life with lessons, stories, and observations that had a tone of insistence in them, each one told in a way that dared me to let it drift from my mind. By the time I turned eleven, I learned of her sister Alva, who cut off two of her husband's fingers, one for each of his mistresses. At twelve, I had no misunderstanding of why, someday soon, for nothing more than a few dollars, I might be stabbed by one of the same boys I played basketball with at the rec center. At thirteen, I came to know that my cousin Dexter hadn't become sick and been hospitalized in St. Louis, but had got a young White girl pregnant and was rumored to be someone's yardman in Hyde Park. And when I was fourteen, through the tree-withering heat of August, during the Watertown Blues Festival, in throngs of sweaty, wide-smiling people, my mother pointed out to me my father.

For the annual festival they closed off Eleventh Street from the downtown square all the way up to where the freight railway cuts through the city, where our neighborhood ends and the land rises up to the surrounding hills, dotted with houses the wealthy built to avoid flooding and neighbors with low incomes. Amidst the summer heat was the sizzle of barbecue at every corner, Blues bands on stages erected in the many empty lots up and down the street, and, of course, scores of people, crammed together, wearing the lightest clothing they could without looking too loose. By early evening the street would be completely filled with people, moving to the Blues.

The sad, slow Blues songs my mother loved the most. The Watertown Festival was her favorite social event of the year. She had a tight-skinned sort of pride through most days of the year, countered by the softer, bare-shouldered self of the Blues Festival, where she wore yellow or orange red outfits and deep, brownish red lipstick against the chestnut shine of her cheeks. More men took notice of her, and every year it was a different man; the summer suitors from past years learned quickly that although she wore that lipstick and although an orange red skirt never looked better on another pair of hips, no man would ever leave another workshirt hanging on her bedpost. With that kind of poise, she swayed through the crowds of people, smiling at many, hugging some, and stopping at times to dance with no one in particular.

When I was younger than fourteen, I had no choice but to

go. Early in the afternoon, she'd make me shower and put on a fresh cotton shirt. *You need to hear the Blues, boy, a body needs something to tell itself what's good and what's not.* At fourteen, my mother approached me differently. She simply came out to the yard where I was watering her garden and said, "You going?" and waited for me to turn to her, and say yes. I didn't know if I liked the Blues or not.

We started at the top of Eleventh Street and worked our way downtown over the few hours of the festival. We passed neighbors and friends from church, my mother's boss from Belk's Dry Goods, and Reverend Riggins, who was drinking beer from a paper cup instead of a can. Midway down Eleventh, in front of Macky's Mellow Tone Lounge, I bumped into my cousin, Wilbert, who had sneaked a tallboy of Miller Hi-Life from a cooler somewhere up the street. A Zydeco band was warming up for Etta James. We stood as still as we could in the intense heat and shared sips of that beer while we watched my mother, with her own beer, swaying with a man twice her age to the zip and smack of the washboard.

Etta James had already captured the crowd when Wilbert brought back a large plate of ribs and another beer. My mother came over to share our ribs, and Wilbert was silent after deftly dropping the can of beer behind his back. I stood there listening, taking in the heat, the music, the hint of beer on my mother's breath. The crowd had a pulse to it, still moving up and down the street but stopping to hear the growl of Etta James's voice. The sense of closeness was almost too much. My mother was swaying back and forth on her heels, giving a little dip to her pelvis every so often and mouthing the words to the songs. At any given moment, one or two men would be looking at her, seemingly oblivious and lost in the music.

But she, too, must have felt the closeness of the people. She was looking away from the stage, focusing on a commotion of laughter in front of Macky's, where voices were hooting above the music. She took hold of my shoulders and turned me towards the front of Macky's. In a circle of loud men, all holding beer, all howling in laughter—some shirtless and others in work clothes—stood a large man in a worn gray suit tugging his tie jokingly like a noose, pushing the men into new waves of laughter each moment. His hair was nappy like he had just risen from bed. But he smiled as if that was never his main concern and he held a presence in that circle of people that made me think he had worn that suit for just such an appearance. My mother held my shoulders tightly for a moment, not tense or angry or anxious, just firm, and then let go.

"There's your father," she said and turned away, drifting back into the music and dancing people. Watching her glide toward the stage, I felt obligated not to follow her. When I could see her no longer, I looked back to the circle of men and the man that my mother had pointed out. From the way he was laughing, he looked like a man who didn't care who he might have bothered with his noise. Certainly his friends didn't seem to mind. Their group commanded a large space of sidewalk in front of the bar. People made looping detours into the crowd instead of walking straight through that wide-open circle of drunken activity. The men stamped their feet, hit each other in the arms and howled as if the afternoon were their own party. I turned to tell Wilbert, but he had gone. I watched the man who was my father slapping his friends' hands, bent over in laughter, sweat soaking his shirt under that suit.

He was a very passionate-looking man, full in his voice, expressively confident in his gestures, and as I watched him, I was thinking of that night fourteen years ago and the lazy thrust of his, that my mother told me had no passion in it at all. I wondered where he must have been all those years and realized how shocked I was to see the real man to fill the image my mother had made. She had made him up for me, but never whole, never fully able to be grasped. I was thinking of his silence, the voice I'd never heard. And wanting nothing else at that moment but to be closer, I walked toward that circle of men. I walked as if I were headed into Macky's Mellow Tone, and they stopped laughing as I split their gathering. The smell of liquor, cheap cologne, and musky sweat hit my nostrils, and I was immediately aware not only that I had no reason for going or chance of getting into Macky's, but that I was also passing through of a circle of strange people. I stopped a few feet from the entrance and focused on the quilted fake leather covering the door's surface. It was faded red fabric, and I looked at that for what seemed a long time because I was afraid to turn back into the men's laughter. The men had started talking again, slowly working themselves back into their own good time. But they weren't laughing at me. I turned to face them, and they seemed to have forgotten that I was there.

I looked up at my father, who was turned slightly away from me. His mouth was open and primed to laugh, but no sound was coming out. His teeth were large, and I could see where sometime before he had lost two of them. Watching him from the street, I had only seen his mouth move and had to imagine what he was saying. Now, so close to him, close enough to smell him, to touch him, I could hear nothing. But I could feel the closeness of the crowd, those unfamiliar men, my father. Then he looked down at me. His mouth closed and suddenly he wasn't grinning. He reached out his hand, and I straightened up as my mother might have told me to do. I arced my hand out to slide across his palm, but he pulled his hand back, smiling—a trickster, like he was too slick for my eagerness.

He reached in his suit jacket and pulled out a pair of sunglasses. Watertown is a small town, and when he put those glasses on he looked like he had come from somewhere else. I know I hadn't seen him before that day. I wondered when in the past few days he must have drifted into town. On what wave of early-morning heat had he arrived?

I looked at myself in the reflection of the mirrored lenses and thought, *So this is me.*

"Them's slick basketball sneakers you got," he said. "I bet you the baddest brother on the court."

I could see only the edge of one eye behind those glasses, but I decided that he was interested.

"Yeah, I am! I'm gonna be like George Gervin, you just watch." And I was sure that after that we'd go inside Macky's and talk. We'd talk about basketball in its entirety and then he'd ask me if I was doing well in school and I'd say not too hot and he'd get on me about that, as if he'd always been keeping tabs on me. Then we would toast to something big, something we could share in the loving of it, like Bill Russell's finger-roll lay-up or the pulled pork sandwich at Ray's Round

Belly Ribs or the fact that I had grown two inches that year even though he wouldn't have known that. We might pause for a moment, both of us quiet, both of us knowing what the silence was about, and he'd look real serious and anxious at the same time, a man like him having too hard a face to explain anything that had happened or hadn't happened. But he'd be trying. He'd say, *hey, brother, cut me the slack, you know how it goes*, and I might say, *it's cool* or I might say nothing at all but know that sometime, later on, we would spend hours shooting hoop together up at the rec center, and when I'd beaten him two out of three at twenty-one, he'd hug me like he'd always known what it was like to love me.

My father took off his sunglasses and looked down at me for a long, silent moment. He was a large man with a square jaw and a wide, shiny forehead, but his skin looked soft—a gentle, light brown. My mother must have believed in his eyes. They were gray—blue, calm, and yet fierce, like the eyes of kinfolk down in Baton Rouge. His mouth was slightly open; he was going to speak and I noticed when I saw him face to face that his teeth were yellow. He wouldn't stop smiling. A thought struck me right then that he might not know who I was.

One of his friends grabbed at his jacket. "Let's roll, brother. Tyree's leavin'!"

He jerked free and threw that man a look that made me stiffen.

The man read his face and then laughed nervously, "Be cool, nigger. Break bad someplace else. We got ladies waitin'."

"I'm cool, brother. I'm cool . . ." My father looked back at me. In the mix of the music and the crowd, which I'd almost forgotten about, I could barely hear him. "I'm cold solid." He crouched down, wiped his sunglasses on a shirttail, and put them in my pocket. His crouch was close. Close enough for me to smell the liquor on his breath. Enough for him to hug me. Close enough for me to know that he wouldn't. But I didn't turn away. I told myself that I didn't care that he was not perfect.

He rose without saying anything else, turned from me, and walked to the corner of Eleventh Street and to the alleyway, where his friends were waiting. They were insistent on him hurrying, and once they were sure that he was going to join them, they turned down the alley. I didn't cry, although I wouldn't have been embarrassed if I had. I watched them leave and the only thing I felt was a wish that my father had never known those men. He started to follow them, but before he left, he stopped to look over the scene there on Eleventh Street. He looked way up the street, to where the crowd thinned out and then beyond that, maybe to where the city was split by the train tracks, running on a loose curve around our neighborhood and to the river, or maybe not as far as that, just a few blocks before the tracks and two streets off Eleventh, where, sometime earlier than fourteen years ago, he might have heard the train's early-morning rumble when he stepped from our back porch.

Kudzu

On that night, years back, we were up until the cardinals started calling. The first one lit out through the leaves before the air went from warm to hot. That call sounded lonely in the quiet of early morning. But soon many of them were fussing in the poplars outside Evvie's porch. Just before it got light, the sharp calls ran all through the dark of the trees. By then we were awake and on the porch. The sky was turning bright behind the kudzu that was taking over the back fence. Evvie had poured more of whatever she was drinking with her coffee and lay lengthwise on the glider. Her ankles were crossed in my lap. When I ran my fingers around each toe, she broke from humming to herself and pulled her lips tight against her teeth. She breathed like the breathing was getting her off. She had breathed like that when she came, hours earlier, when I had her bent over the back of the glider on her porch.

That's how she makes me say it now, *bent over, entered from behind*, like we're a coroner's report. She doesn't like it if I say, *doggie style*. When I first caught up with her today, I tried that out, just to joke, like we used to do, but she looked dead at me and sucked her teeth. *It ain't like that now*, she said, no shame in her face. Evvie tells me not to say things like *sweetmeat* and *assfuck*. She says she'd rather not talk about sex at all. But years back, when I massaged her feet, she dribbled her drink, opened her mouth, and let her neck go slack. Her teeth were slick with the wet of her tongue. And I figured all that had to do with me.

But there was a lot to that night. The sun had been down a while and the sky was still bright with red and purple, like the whole dusk was swollen. The air was wet and the thick clouds clung close to the hills. Like early morning, those birds were carrying on. And when we first got to Evvie's place, the cicadas were buzzing as it got dark. *You know what that's all about*, Evvie would say. It sounds like spring works from inside your middle. Even now, that buzz goes through me everywhere at once. By early morning we'd been at it all over the house: couch, rocker, hallway floor, twice in the bathtub.

Later, we sat in the mist as it blew across her porch. The scent of turned earth was on the air. I was thinking that the wind was horny, just like everything else in early June. Breeze blew through where the kudzu was thick enough to round the sharp corners of the fence. The wind pushed the vines from their tangle and fanned them out into the yard. When the kudzu moved like that, it looked like something large and hungry was rolling around inside. Sometimes I imagined there was something scrambling through the vines. Sometimes I was sure there was: a dog or a man, looking for some stash they dug or threw back in there. But nothing was ever there. Just breeze through vine. There was a hum to the breeze, a soft heave from the greenery. Above where the vines covered the top of the fence, the night was near quiet, but had a low sigh, just like that heave. And above all of that we could hear the Bensons, her upstairs neighbors, fucking again.

We listened to their couch scoot in short scrapes along the floor above Evvie's front room ceiling. The Bensons were both talkers. They made love the way they argued. He was *sweetie's big daddy, she was his fat-back baby*, on and on like that. Day was coming, and they were wearing out their front-room couch. We could hear them from her porch, in the back of the building. I was nodding in and out of sleep. But Evvie listened. She had her lips open, and for a moment she held her breath. In the stillness, she went stiff, and all we could hear was Mrs. Benson: *you gettin' it now, sugar. It's right there . . . get it right there!* Something splintered and shook the ceiling. And Evvie let out her breath.

When I ask her about that now, she says she was sighing back to the night air.

"I used to do things like that," she says.

"You still do," I say, like I have any idea what she's doing now.

She smiles at this, sips on her drink, looks along the bar. There's a downward turn to her lips, like whatever she's looking at in this place disappoints her. She hasn't been here for a while. Macky's Mellow Tone Lounge is the same as it was three years ago. Padded vinyl bar and tables, six wooden booths, the same color as the red that Dessa, the owner, painted the whole place. Even before Dessa took over, I never knew the inside of Macky's to have another color. It was a narrow room with a long bar. Beer signs between pictures of Booker T, Dr. King, and Garvey; Nancy Wilson above the jukebox. There wasn't a bar display, liquor bottles lit up and all that, but if you asked for something, Dessa would pour it. The jukebox never played new tunes, but stopped playing the oldest, about one album at a time. I brought Evvie by here to see the fellas, shout *hey* to Dessa.

Evvie gets up to pick songs on the jukebox and it's only then that I see what I couldn't make sense of when we bumped into each other earlier. She looks like she never came from here: head wrap, bangles, toe rings, and something like a sheet or a big robe brushing the tops of her feet.

"It's a kaftan," she says when Dessa stares long enough.

"Your money, not mine," is all Dessa says.

I ran into Evvie at the barber's. I go once every two weeks. She was walking out of Willie's shop when I was walking in. When she closed the door, the whole room was busting out in laughter. It was like she had never left Watertown. I heard her voice first, a laugh that's deep from in her chest and loose, wide mouthed, like a child's. I expected to see her in nursing scrubs. She used to spend half her days in them. When I'd pick her up from her shift we'd go straight to Macky's, and although the fellas saw me with her, looking like that, it didn't matter to me. She wore thong underwear underneath. *Just for you, baby*, she used to tell me. She knew I liked that kind of secret. Three years since I'd seen that woman.

When I ran into her outside Willie's, I saw that kaftan covering her and wondered what was under all that. Somewhere in there was her body, but when I tried to give her a hug, she didn't let me hold her long, so I got more cloth than hip. I couldn't feel if she was bigger or more bony. Before anything else I said, *let's drink something*. We walked to the car as quiet as prom dates. We were silent most of the way to the bar.

I stole glances at her while I was driving. She watched the streets go by. She was fanning the hem of the kaftan between her knees. *Still don't have air conditioning.* She laughed out the window. *Most folks wear less when the sun's out*, I said, and she sucked her teeth, rolled her eyes, gave me that shows-what-you-know look. The next time I looked she had the hem pulled to her thighs. There was a scar of raised skin along the outside of her knee. She had been an athlete—volleyball, basketball, track—the baby girl in a house of three brothers over six feet. The knee gave out on her at Regionals; the slower girl she had just beat to the basket fell on her leg. A year later, she won the Tennessee State Finals for long jump. The skin around that scar ran to her thigh; her muscles were taut, like she was always ready to sprint. *It's been a while since I saw that*, I said, *what else you hiding?* She was looking out the window, letting the air rushing past the car push against her palm. When she turned to me, I was trying to laugh, but she wasn't smiling.

She was the one who first got me talking that way. Hints and taunts that led to clothes on the kitchen floor and sweat on the counters. That's what I wanted to say after we had our drinks and found a booth in Macky's. Years back, she liked to tell me to tell her what I wanted to do. I tried to talk the way she wanted. At first, I wasn't that creative. We'd get a few drinks in us and I'd push the dishes into the sink so we could use the counter. *I hope you're ready, baby*, I'd say, and when she'd say, *I've been wet since you pulled out this morning*, I would smile like a wallflower until I could think of what to say next.

As I got smoother with the smooth talk, I'd leave messages on her beeper when she was on lunch break, something like, *Don't be wearing nothing but oil when I get home*. I did it just for laughs. But she'd knock off work a bit early and be sitting on her front porch with a robe on and a glass of rum by the time I got there. Or I'd see a note on her screen door *got your message* and I could smell sandalwood oil drifting from inside, like the whole house was waiting for me. For a while it was good like that.

Not long after, the Bensons moved in upstairs. The first time we met them, they were going at it outside Evvie's apartment. We heard them before we saw them; from the parking lot, they sounded like somebody was wrestling on the stairs to the upper floors. We walked up the steps to Evvie's door and there they were, in the stairwell. Her high heels were in the middle of the landing. We said *ev'nin'* and he pulled his hand from her skirt. They nodded back. He patted her ass with the heels as they went up the stairs.

They played the same record all night. Koko Taylor, on into the early hours. The Bensons were louder than their stereo. Whatever got them horny got into us too. That night, Evvie and I almost broke her dining room table. After a month, it was like that every weekend, two or three times on Saturdays alone. Evvie got to listening for them: If I was fucking her, hearing them pushed her to yelling herself. Or if it was some time between the last and the next time I was fucking her, she started touching herself.

After a few weeks of that, she would put her hand over my mouth when I got to telling her how I was going to do her. *Listen*, she would say, and gaze at the ceiling. Above, Mr. Benson was making damn sure Mrs. Benson knew who her ass belonged to, or Mrs. Benson was letting Mr. Benson know damn well where her sugarbowl was: *no, baby, you just watch this time, watch how I do it*. Evvie's eyes would be closed, her hand over my mouth, her legs going tight, quivering into her own good time. *You just watch how I do myself*. Because they went at it late at night, we were up, too. By the time the sun was shining from the front room down the hall, we were on Evvie's back patio with the glider cushions spread out on the deck. The Bensons would be just above where her bedroom let onto the patio. Before the paper hit the front porch, we had been back in the shower and sweaty all over again on her front room couch.

Unless they were going out for drinks, Mrs. Benson was always home, playing Carla Thomas forty-fives over the rattle of a sewing machine. I never did figure out what Mr. Benson did.

It got to be that we spent most nights at Evvie's. Late at night I would wake up to the carrying-on upstairs. Sometimes what they said didn't make sense. Just shouting and hollering. I'd wake out of dreams and wonder what the hell was I hearing. From my dream it sounded like somebody's pet locked in a closet, but then I'd hear her say, *Got damn, Ronnie, get it, baby*, something like that, and I'd remember what it was. I'd look to see if Evvie was asleep and her eyes would be wide open to the ceiling. On some nights she would mouth whatever it was the Bensons said most often. When I finally said to her, *you never bust out when we get it on like that*, she said, *we never get it on like that*.

After a few weeks, I wasn't sleeping over there. We didn't argue or get cold with each other. It just seemed like more nights we slept or listened to the Bensons. Then it was more nights we either fell asleep, or I wasn't over there. Eventually, Evvie stopped calling every day and I found myself at Macky's most weekends, watching the ball game. I told myself it was because the Braves were good that year. A few months later, folks stopped seeing Evvie around town. When Dessa finally asked me where Evvie had run off to, I said west. That's all her phone message said. Dessa said, *that ain't too damn specific*, and I said, *that's Evvie*.

Some weeks after that I ran into Mr. Benson at Macky's. He was running nine-ball over some kid who didn't have sense enough not to bring his two weeks' pay to a bar. Mr. Benson didn't say much more than, *which hole you want me to put the nine, son?* Mr. Benson was one of those brothers stuck in 1983: dressed sharp in leisure suit combos and two-color Stacy Adams patent leathers, blue tinted eyeglasses, Jheri curls long in back, close above his ears. Between games he'd lean into the bar while Dessa freshened up his Johnnie Walker.

I eased up, yelled to Dessa, *I got his, and pour me double whatever it is this brother drinks*. He looked my way, saw that we knew each other, and turned back to stare at himself in the mirror that ran along the bar. I told his reflection, *if it's the drink that keeps your lady and mine up at night, I gotta try some of that shit*. Mr. Benson tipped his glass to our reflections in the long bar mirror before he turned to the pool table and said, *it ain't the drank*.

After that he ran five games of nine-ball on me. He spoke only to call a pocket or ball combination. When he was done, and I had bought him a double at the bar, he tipped his glass to the mirror and smiled a smoker's yellow-tooth grin, *the lady just likes what I got and likes it a long time.* He didn't say another word, and I didn't ask anything else.

Evvie looks like she wants to go. We haven't said much—traded news about friends and laughed a little about my brick-head nephews. She gets up to put more money in the jukebox.

"The Teddy Pendergrass don't play no more," Dessa shouts, "you wore that out, Evvie."

Evvie lets out that wide-mouth laugh. She bends over, like she's going to laugh herself to the floor. Her hands go to her waist, and I can see where her hips begin. For a minute I think maybe the head wrap and kaftan are a joke and any moment she's going to throw that off and ask me to dance close, my thigh between hers, and it won't matter what's playing on the jukebox. She sees me watching. She watches me sitting at the edge of the booth, like I might get up.

"You still funny, girl," Evvie says to Dessa, and by the time she's back to the booth, her smile is gone.

We sit for a while, waiting for Dessa's sorry jukebox to find something that plays. I can hear the empty record slots, click-ing, clicking. Evvie keeps her eyes to the street.

When I ask her where she's been all this time, she tells me that she's been travelling.

"I just drove," she says.

"*Drove* another brother crazy, right?" I laugh.

She isn't laughing. "Drove west. Drove north. Away from here," she says.

"Lookin' for your gold-tooth sugar daddy."

"See, that's your problem," she says, "got shit figured out before you know shit about it."

I don't say anything to this.

"Maybe if you paid attention some of the time, you'd have some damn sense."

Now it's me who feels like leaving.

She tells me how for a long time she didn't call anybody in Watertown, or any of her kin in Tennessee. Months before she left, she took to saying, *I live in Watertown, but it don't live in me.* Bars and beauty salons were the only happening places around where we lived. Beyond that, Watertown was rail yards, half of downtown boarded up, industrial parks and neighborhoods where White folks only allowed us in to clean. Once a year, the city would put on a Blues festival on Eleventh Street—five bands, barbeque, cold beer and card games all day—and folks would almost get to thinking that there wasn't much else to look forward to. When she had enough, Evvie drove the hell out of here.

I ask her whose bed she was sleeping in all this time.

"Didn't matter where I woke up," she says, "motel, parked in a campground, somebody's couch. Nights were just me, by myself. That got to feeling good. Wasn't nobody next to me but me." Then she looks dead at me. "Whose bed was I in? You mean who was I *fucking*. You really got to know that?" And then she told me more than I wanted to know. At first she was using her fingers. Then she tried some toys. She took an art class, made something out of clay, thick with ridges; it had a curve to it, and she thought that was like me, but after a while, she said she didn't need it. Threw it away in a Waffle House dumpster.

She made her way farther south than Watertown. South, she says, just south. Maybe it was in Georgia where she found a way to stay in somebody's house for a while. She didn't say if they were kin or not. Just a house in the middle of trees and heat. She would walk the swamps, gig for fish, gather wood. She didn't say how she paid for things, but after some months she burned her scrubs and nursing shoes in a trash can.

"Thongs, too," she tells me, like that's the part I should laugh at.

After all of that, I try to lighten things up. When I ask Evvie who she's fucking now, she doesn't answer right away. She sucks her teeth again, pats her head wrap, looks at her hands.

"I didn't have no place or nobody. I had my car key, *one key,* on my chain for a whole year," and when she says *chain* there's a drop in her voice like I haven't heard since she called four-thirty, some Sunday morning, early in the first year after she left town. She had her drink on: loud, sassy, sloppy. In the background, I could hear a car engine rumbling. Maybe it was a truck. I could hear wind blowing like it came from some cold as hell place. She was yelling at me. She'd go on for a while and I'd try to say something to calm her, but I didn't try to say all that much. It was four-thirty in the morning.

In the background, I could hear some woman laughing a sludge-thick smoker's heave that begins with a chuckle and ends with that shit they never hack up. It seemed to me that this woman knew Evvie. *Fuck that nigga, Evvie,* she kept laughing. I couldn't tell if she was laughing at me, like she had me figured, or just laughing at Evvie, drunk on the phone and yelling at some man in Tennessee. She probably had that figured, too. I tried to tell Evvie to call me back when she was alone. She told me she was getting free of her chain, all those *goin nowhere* brothers. When I asked her what did all that have to do with me, there was a silence on the line. I could hear her breathing hard against the cold where she was. After a while, I hung up.

When Al Green comes on the jukebox, I say, "That's my jam" and I get up to get us more drinks. From the bar I watch her mouthing the words. She looks out the window, to Eleventh Street: folks walking from downtown, work to home, brothers gathered outside the bar, shit-talking about last night's game. She lets her head bop a little, a small sway of her hand back and forth in the air, like she's a backup singer. The song fades and she's still looking out the window. I stand at the bar longer than I should, but she never looks my direction. Dessa comes from behind the bar to have a smoke. She's looking at Evvie, too.

"What did you do to that girl?" She laughs.

I don't know what to tell Dessa. Last time I thought I had Evvie figured out, cardinals were calling.

In the Swamp

for James Alan McPherson

I figure my fiancée wants to know why I haven't explained myself. We have just driven south for two days to stand in the back of a funeral parlor. Cherise has no idea why I wanted to go back to my hometown for the funeral of a man she has never heard me speak of. Our drive back north is quiet as the first changes of fall rush past. Tulip poplars are nearing yellow, and the maple has already gone red. If she asked, I could look along the slopes of the Smoky Mountains and tell her which color belongs to which tree, how long before what's yellow turns orange, when what's red fades to brown. But small talk about autumn isn't going to cut it.

A man I once knew died in Watertown. I made a last-minute drive to a place I haven't been in ten years, because that's what I had to do. She wanted to come, to be with me, she said. Calvin Powell is dead and buried now, and until five days ago, Cherise never knew he existed. *So, this Cal?* she would ask if I explained more than I have already, *what was up with him?* There is so much of Watertown I try not to think about—less that I want to share—but, just now, as I look at Cherise, I see that she knows less of me than she would like.

Until six days ago, as far as I was concerned, Cal Powell *didn't* exist. I was at work when a high school friend I hadn't thought of in years called to say Cal's heart gave out while he was driving someplace. I looked out my office window to the flat, gray wall of Boston sky and said his name: *Calvin Powell,* the same way I catch myself in the middle of meetings, mumbling the names of rivers—*Suck Creek, Chattahoochie, Nantahala*—because if you pass years without speaking a name, you can come to think that maybe there was nothing to that name. *Calvin Delrose Powell.* The bass of it was thick in the back of my mouth. I said it again and again—*Calvin Delrose Powell*—and he was dead, then alive for a moment, and then dead.

I don't know what I will tell Cherise, but I pull the car to the side of the road. She isn't surprised by the stop and her shoulders relax into the seat. The sun warms the cinnamon brown of her face, and though her jaw is slack with calm, her eyes shift from the road to the fields, to the sky, to her hands. It's her way of looking irritated. Her hair is cut short and she looks like the proud-faced child I have seen in photographs on her parent's mantel. A few strands hide those eyes, looking at everything but me. She is waiting to hear what I have to say. It's damn time I started explaining what she doesn't know, why this quick drive south, why I did not make an effort to speak to anyone at the funeral, why no one spoke to us, why I have said very little to her in three days.

"I'm not going to get into all of it now," I tell her, "it would take more than a few days' drive for that. Sometimes you have to see something laid to rest. I went to see Cal put in the ground. Let some things settle for good." And I want to say more, but I pause, thinking of what to include in the story I might tell her.

Cherise came up in a house where her parents talk through their problems and enjoy recounting the stories of their past— what was embarrassing is made endearing, what was painful, they romanticize their having endured it. Though she has never said it, I know she feels she and I should share in everything. After all, we are getting married, someday. We are engaged, without a wedding day in mind. This should be the time when we grow together, and yet this is where I am stuck: not in loving her and that proud-girl beauty of hers, but in what I share of myself. What to tell, what to remember, what not to tell. I didn't come up like she did.

If I tell her anything more than what I have, I will tell her about when I was seventeen, when Cal was foreman for my summer job at Weyerhardt Steel and I was spending more hours out of my house than in. We lived just outside town, where fifteen years of my mother's savings as a cleaning woman secured two acres and a two-story, three-bedroom house. It was just my mother and me, and had been like that for as long as I could remember. I never knew my father and though I'd get the questions about where my daddy was, I was never bothered by who or where that man was. If asked, I would answer that he lived in Memphis, and that was as far as I went with it.

Other than the folks we saw at church and the neighbors Momma traded across-the-fence pleasantries with, I never knew Momma to have friends. For some reason, what friends I had never came by the house. It did not seem like the thing to do. Momma was always startled by neighbors who dropped by unannounced. Her voice would be pleasant and measured as she offered them sweet tea, but her tone was never welcoming.

When I was much younger, Momma would take me when she cleaned other people's homes rather than leave me with a sitter. If it was warm out, she would sit me on a porch or in a backyard with crayons and paper. She had a portable radio and she would set it near me while she cleaned inside. On colder days, she would set me up in a kitchen, same crayons, paper, and radio. Every once in a while, she would come to check on me, a look through the door, or call from the top of some stairs, but never a touch on the head or a moment to take up a crayon to add to what planes, bears, and racing cars I had doodled.

My teenage years felt much the same: Momma from a distance, calling me for supper, sending me to the yard for chores, wishing me good night from behind a closed door. No time together spent watching television or playing dominoes. Momma wasn't like that. She was a proud, calm-faced woman, with hard, distant eyes that never rested on you for long.

There were men at church who tried getting close to her after service, but other than pastor and Cal Powell, I remember few men coming to our home.

Before he was my ride to work, Cal was the man Momma would call when our trees needed pruning, when the water pump went out, septic line backed up, things like that. Momma had a strong back and strong hands. She could fix the furnace and change the oil in the car, but there were some jobs she wouldn't do. She didn't mind Cal's prices, either: a fifth of Wild Turkey, half-dozen jars of peaches or pickled beets. Cal had been coming to our house for years, but in late spring of my seventeenth year, I saw more of him than I had been used to.

When I was younger—eight or nine—Cal would take me fishing, and as I grew into my teens, to minor-league games. Momma didn't mind. Cal took to me like a friend, and by the time I was seventeen, I had shared more than a few beers with him on fishing trips and in bleacher seats. He knew how to time a joke. Knew about fish, birds, land and trees, engines, and dogs. He could tell better than anybody else how Ronnie Sours hit a ball clean out of Ferris Field, something nobody, except for Harmon Killebrew, had done before or since.

I had been working the foundry job two weeks into June when I first heard Cal's Dodge rumbling up our drive, twenty minutes before he was supposed to pick me up for work. He talked to Momma on the porch while I ate my breakfast. Come Monday the next week, he was at the table when I came down to eat. The house smelled of the fresh biscuits and sausage gravy that were on the table but the whole kitchen smelled of Aqua-Velva. I had watched the man choke down three ham sandwiches during our fifteen-minute afternoon break, but Cal ate those biscuits slowly, chewing on one side of his mouth, then the other, like each bite mattered. Momma made fresh biscuits for him every morning that week.

On Friday morning, he pushed from the table to go, leaned over to Momma, and said, "Biscuits so good, I might carry that boy to work Saturday, Sunday, Christmas, New Year's, Easter, Juneteenth, too." He got up, left out the back door. It took me a week to notice that Momma had a faint hue of dark red glossing her brown lips and the hairnet she wore most mornings was nowhere to be seen.

By the end of June he was spending his evenings at the house. We might sit at the kitchen table or in the Florida room, glass louvers open, eating fried catfish and listening to the radio. I used to think the thing between them was about the way they talked late into the night, the stolen glances they shared as we cleared dinner plates, or the way they sat together on the porch: Momma leaning into him, swaying to what was on the radio, her elbows on her knees, then reaching to sip at his bourbon. Long after I had gone upstairs, I could hear them from my room, their soft laughter rising through the canopy of poplars that stood just outside my window.

One early July morning after such an evening, I rose to hear Momma singing. When I came downstairs she was on the back porch, pressing pleats into a dress I had never seen her wear. The house smelled of biscuits. I don't remember what I said, something to tease her about how late they were up, and I remember her laughing out loud, just as she had with Cal. She looked off to the edge of the yard, and I was thinking to myself that maybe that weekend she might come with us to a ball game. Ball games, fried corn and catfish, dominoes on the porch, Albert King on the radio. Maybe the summer was going to be like that. Momma and I were laughing together, something that did not happen often. I was not one to crack jokes with her, but hearing her laugh right then, I felt like I could. I smiled and said to Momma, "You should see yourself, laughing like a girl in high school."

But then she stopped grinning. She looked at me for a moment and then took the dress into the kitchen before she was done pressing it. I didn't know what I had said. But in that moment I realized there were parts of her I would never know.

A week later, I woke on a Saturday morning to hear Momma yelling, something she rarely did, especially not in the middle of the driveway. I certainly never heard her yell at Cal.

"I got troubles as it is, don't need yours too, not in my house, not around my boy."

I heard Cal's truck start up, and watched from my window as he drove off. My mother watched him from the yard. He didn't come around the house at all the following week, and instead picked me up for work at the corner.

On Friday night, Cal and I picked up our routine: a plate of ribs and a ball game, and I was thinking that whatever had happened with Momma and him might soon cool off. But as he took me home Cal pulled his truck to the side of the road that led to my house. I wondered if he planned to let me off at the corner, where he picked me up for work.

When I asked him why he hadn't been around, he started with, "Your mother . . ." caught himself, and didn't say another word about it. Then he turned the truck around and said "Let's get us some dranks," and drove toward Ephron's Market.

I never knew for sure why he stopped coming around. If I had asked Momma about it, she'd have said it was not for me to know. She never let anyone get too close for too long.

I was only seventeen, but Cal and I had spent time that June in bars along Eleventh Street, out in the sticks, in backroad garages and barns, where beer sat in coolers under engine blocks and bald-felt pool tables. He bounced his rusted-out Dodge all over the county. I didn't mind riding around with him. I didn't want to go to my house either.

It was very late, if not already early. The heat of the day had long given up, and the air was sweet, the way it is at four in the morning, when only drunks and lovers take notice. Wind pushed at the trees without a sound, and the scent of black locust and new hay discs blew across the fields. Mist hung in the culverts and along the tree lines. The wetlands were the dark nothing beyond. We were nearing the bridge at Donahue's Field, which used to graze cattle before it was a dump on the edge of swampland. Now it held the American Legion softball diamonds. When we crossed the bridge, Cal was griping about how the Braves would never take the pennant.

One moment he was going on and on about "back in the Henry Aaron days . . ." over the truck tires hitting the steel span of the bridge and then he hit the brakes.

I steadied myself on the dash and turned to see what had happened. Cal heaved air like something had burst in his chest. He tried to smile, the way folks do when they want to avoid crying. He was built the way folks were before machines did most of their work. Not tall, but thick. Small head, wide back, satisfied belly. You could see the strength in his hands, like he could work rivets into place without a jack. But right then, he looked like a scared boy, poised to set off running.

Everything was still, and for a moment I lost a sense of where I was. Cal whispered something, a word—maybe he said it twice—then he shuddered and his shoulders locked up. If I knew back then how seizures can take a body like a bullet, I might have thought he was having one. I might have eased him to the passenger's side of the cab, and hurried on to his house or to a hospital, but instead I just watched.

He turned away and looked out past the patches of grass in the swamp stream. Maybe I heard an early cardinal; maybe I wanted to. Frogs called from down the stream. The Dodge was idling.

"Let's get on," he said and slowly pulled off. The headlights flickered across paved road. We turned a corner. He looked ahead into the blue band of night over the swamp, and the glow from town lit his face.

"That field . . ." he said.

"What? Donahue Field?" I was quick to answer back.

He was quiet for a moment. He said, "Back in sixty-seven somebody tole me they buried a whole mess a tires under that field, in part of the landfill where it used to be swamp. You got these tires, right? They's rubber. Just work they way back up. Flat ball field turned to lumps. Had to come in with heavy equipment to lay that field right." He rubbed one palm on his thigh, switched with his steering hand, and did the same with the other. "Some things just do like that."

By then, he was driving fast. I could only watch him, leaning one arm out the window, face shifting from the glint of far-off lights. He was saying something, but I couldn't hear him. Then he looked at me, and I felt like I was supposed to say something, but I didn't. We just rode around. I can't call the names of roads we crossed. I remember that we were quiet.

After driving like that for a half hour or so we came up on Ephron's Market. The Snacks—Tackle—Beer sign glowed over the dark fields. He turned into the lot and stopped.

Cal smiled at me, rubbed his face, and said "Miller time," as if it was Saturday afternoon and we had bleacher seats and a bucket of fried chicken at Fulton County Stadium.

I watched him walk through the cloud of moths buzzing

the bulb above the gas pumps. He blurred into the flashes the moth wings made as they swarmed under the lamp. He stood there a moment and looked up into the swirl of soft sparks before stepping out of the circle of light. I heard the bell tinkle as he walked into the store and shouted, "Hey, Sammy Eff, how much for a free beer?"

I thought back to weeks ago when we were out fishing and he spoke of towns and people he knew. He had been places. Picked up and left, gone, lived some life, and come back. I had known only Watertown, the roads around it, Momma and me, alone in that house. Cal talked to me like an old travelling companion, reminiscing on places as if we had both been off, looking for things to get into. Once that beer got in him he would get wound up in one of his stories about the women he'd known.

"There weren't many, but what there was, I give 'em what all I got," he said. But he had loved only one. He spoke about her the least, out of respect for Momma. He never told me much more than the way this woman laughed, the dress she looked good in, how she cooked greens better than his momma's. He'd catch himself before he said too much. When I asked Momma about her, she said that Glenda Kendricks had left town, without a word, sometime in spring of that year, a month or so before Cal became more than a handyman around our house. No one knew for certain what day she actually cut out of Watertown. She was the sort of lady nobody knew well but saw around the way, at church and in bars, walking Eleventh Street, where folks assumed she lived.

Momma said the story about Calvin Powell and Glenda Kendricks took all types of family, friends, postal carriers, barbershop tales, and after-church gossip to build up to anything people couldn't settle in their minds themselves. No one wanted to tell a story about her just up and gone, no goodbye, no reason. People wanted to figure out why, like something in them wouldn't be settled if they didn't get it right.

After she was gone folks put Glenda Kendricks all over the South and as far west as Galveston: She went looking for her first love; some man come to town in a smoke gray Lincoln, waving money around, and off she went; she took a bus for Texas, looking for a child she gave up when she was young. I never knew which story to fix on. Momma said she knew of Glenda, but she didn't like to speak of somebody the way folks did.

"People get to forgetting or recalling as it suits them," she would say. "Time somebody re-remember you in and out of the story they got working in their own mind, it ain't hardly you."

The boys at the foundry told me Cal kept a picture of a lady in his wallet, but if they asked about her, all he'd say was "jus my ole used-to-be," and that was as much as he would say.

In the truck at Ephron's, Cal gone to get beer, I leaned back, lost in what had happened out by the field. He looked scared when he told me about the tires, but before the tires he had mumbled something else. And as Cherise and I now sit on the side of the road, it comes to me like a small, sharp echo: *Glenda*.

Cal came back to the truck, and we drove to a pond to drink beer and talk into early morning. More than talk, there was the dark, cloudless sky, the slick, black pond, and the company of night things. It sounded like a world of cicadas and frogs. I said something about those sounds, slipping into echoes across the water. He said nothing. I tried to catch a look at his eyes as I gave him a beer, but he turned and walked to sit on his heels at the water's edge. I followed and stood a few feet behind him. Half his beer was gone in one draw, and he threw the bottle toward deep water. It spun away from us, end over end, foam trailing, glass sparkling in the glow from town lights, before splashing in the shadows. We stared out to where it hit and we were silent for a while, like that meant something.

"Bottles. Stay put where they sink. Now those tires," I said, trying to make some connection to what I thought startled him earlier that night, "they don't stay down, sounds like. Piles of tires," but I wasn't sure of what I was saying. "Seen shit like that, brother, thrown all the hell everywhere. A world of mosquitos up in there, waitin' to put the sting on your ass." And I laughed because I wanted it to be funny.

"It ain't just about tires," he said. "The swamp, it moves things. Everybody throw they shit in there. You throw something in there, never give a care for it again, and up it come someplace else."

I thought I understood him. The swamp was strange that way. It was a wide stretch of bottomland, scarred with stands of pond pine, oak, and sycamore. It wasn't a real swamp, not like in Louisiana, but it smelled like swamp, sucked at your feet like swamps do. From a plane, the swamp wasn't much, but walk in it for a while and the land got large. It felt like a swamp, so that's what we called it.

Folks from way back used to dig graves on the solid land back in there, the only burial land left for them, but most would tell you it was so the poplar and dogwood they planted there would thrive. Over the years, farmers graded the land around the swamp, put in landfill, planted crops, harvested, turned the soil. Rivers and waterways shifted, pushed and pulled at the soil. People worked the land more than they watched how it washed away.

A thought would get into somebody that they should visit the family plot. They would go to pay their respects and find their plot gone. Some would find a keeling headstone, displaced yards into the pond. Some might find only the ten-year-old tupelo they last saw when it was a sapling. The older men still talk on the porch of Ephron's about a rainy summer before T.V.A. dams, when Ellard Williams was moving fieldstones on the edge of his land and found somebody's rib cage.

All of us had known of something lost and found near the swamp. I wanted to say this, but I felt like Cal wouldn't hear it right, like I was just mixing his mess in with everybody else's. I was seventeen and on summer vacation. I just let it go.

At some point I finally said, "We best be getting on."

He took his time throwing stones into dark water.

I tried to nudge him, and he stood up fast enough so that I stepped back. He was swaying. I figured he was drunk. I reached out to steady him, and he took hold of my thumb. He bent it toward my wrist, and pain flared from my hand to my shoulder. We looked dead at each other a moment. His grip loosened, and he eased me back a step. After he had taken a few steps toward the truck, I followed.

I said, "It's just getting late, that's all. You know how folks always worry."

And he said, "Not always."

We were quiet as he drove me home. The swamp felt larger around us, and I was eager to get out of it. Cal had told me a long while ago that the only people who knew their way in the swamp were runaway slaves and their children, who found a way to live back in there. It was the one place, besides hundreds of miles north and west, that master wouldn't follow. More than a hundred years gone, there were still people who went into the swamp to hunt, to live, hide from the law, or hide something that wouldn't be found. I felt like I was hearing everything around us at a volume louder than things needed to be—tires on the road, raccoon and possum rustling through Johnson grass, calls of what I wanted to be birds, but could imagine as people, lost and wandering the dark.

When he let me out at my house, he didn't say a word. I stepped to the porch and turned to watch the glow from the truck's running lights pull away. That was a Friday, and we didn't speak over the weekend. He wasn't at Sunday service. On Monday, he missed his first day at the foundry in ten years. That Thursday I heard they found him in the swamp.

He was stooped over, breathing hard, shirt dried stiff with sweat, his arms and legs stuck in the mud. He'd been out there for a day or so before an old man poaching dove came up on him. If the man hadn't been ducking the game warden, he would never have seen Cal in such a tucked-away place.

"Damn fool was bent over; had his arms all jammed into the mud," the man told the fellas at Ephron's. "Like he was lookin' for somethin'."

All that I heard about Cal was through the boys at the barbershop and the older men who held court on the front porch of Ephron's. The hospital released him within a day. They said he was a strong man for his fifties; all he needed was water and rest. But he didn't go back to work.

By then Momma had made me quit the plant job. She said I had saved enough of my pay to take the rest of the summer off. Soon I would be off to college, she told me, and it would be good to be closer to home before I was gone. The next to last thing I heard about Cal was that the plant fired him so that he could draw unemployment. The last thing I heard about him was that he went into Macky's Lounge for one bourbon and a beer, and was rarely seen in town for weeks after. I remember being relieved, not because he had been found or that he wasn't dead, but because I did not want to see the man ever again.

When Cherise and I were first driving south, my best explanation was that I had to go to the funeral because I hadn't thought of Cal in years. I tried to explain about how remembering him was like naming a river—a hill, the street you grew up on, folks you laughed with—just so that you know you came from somewhere. With all that in my head, I tried to tell her how it takes me some time to remember where I came from.

But Cherise is a tax lawyer who knows a thing or two about selective memory, and she was quick to point out that "you never speak of your mother, and she isn't a damn river." And I didn't have an answer for that.

I sit in the car with my fiancée. I touch her wrist and draw in the breath that I think is going to push me to start talking to her. She's shared enough of my life in restaurants and bars, up and down grocery aisles, on vacations to Oak Bluff and laughing with her family in Springfield to feel she knows me. She looks at me, her face at first soft, like she's eager to understand when I tell her not just about Cal Powell but more about me. Who are my people? That's what she wants. I smile as if I'm about to explain just that, but I'm silent, and the lines in her face go tight. She thinks I'm all bullshit. She gets out of the car, sits on the hood, then walks to the bridge. The car is running, I'm sitting in it, and even if I could explain what I haven't told her about my family, something in me wants to hold onto it for myself.

In my mother's house there was never talk of my father or how Momma left him, asleep in an East St. Louis duplex in the middle of the night, bound for family in Knoxville—me in the backseat of a bus, confused at five years old, but sure by morning that Illinois was far enough away that we wouldn't be going back. I remember nothing of the months we lived in Knoxville. And I soon forgot the family that didn't chase after Momma when she moved on to Watertown before that year was out. I knew our distant family only as faces floating in the pictures my mother kept until I was seventeen.

One day, without a word, she got rid of them. August was almost gone, and it had been weeks since Cal Powell drove his truck out of our driveway. Momma didn't talk about him or any other man. It was a Saturday, and she had me folding blankets in the attic for summer storage. There was just enough light from the dormer window to see dust drift across the cedar panels that lined the attic. After the blankets, I was to wipe down the kitchen baseboards.

I was done with the blankets much earlier than Momma had planned. I lay on top of the trunk and watched the dust drift from the dark of the cedar paneling into the hazy light glowing through the dormer window. I dozed in and out until the light outside quickly faded. Streamers of gray smoke blocked out the sun as I stepped to the window. I looked down to the yard, where the smoke churned from an oil drum we used to burn garbage and cuttings. Momma was next to the can. She tore pages from large books and threw them over the small fire. The pages held photographs, which curled against the fire rising in the can.

I recognized the books, three clothbound albums Momma had wrapped in a gingham tablecloth and held on her lap when we took the bus from Knoxville to Watertown. I didn't know all the names of the people in the pictures, but I knew they were family.

Even now, all I know of family was what I saw in those photographs: twig of crepe myrtle stuck in a baby's wicker bassinette, a pinkie ring on a young soldier, the pomade and stocking cap waves in an uncle's hair, if he was an uncle at all. In the back of the third album Momma had begun to paste in pictures of us: Cal, her, and me, pictures that, unlike any other photographs, she labelled: *Cal cleaning fish, lucky catch . . . The boys fixing (and breaking) the car. Cal and me, off to the movies.* I had taken the shot before the movies. Cal had been to the barber's. He held a straw porkpie with a new grosgrain band. Momma's dress was a simple cotton, but she had pressed it with starch three times. She smiled the same smile I saw in pictures from her childhood.

Just as I came to realizing that it was photos she was tossing, Momma tossed a jar of clear liquid over the photos and I could hear the flames explode from where I stood inside the attic. By the time I reached the second floor, coils of black smoke raced past the landing window. By the time I reached the yard, there was nothing left of the books but flames and thick smoke. A gasoline flash fire, it burned fierce and quick like a match before I could get the hose, and then nothing.

Momma parted her lips to a nervous smile. She spread the sweat from her face to press back her hair. Right then, she felt less like my mother and more simply like a woman I had seen but never known, observed for years in church or along the aisles of the grocery store. I saw in her the girl of photos from her younger years in Knoxville, a big-eyed girl whose slim smile didn't hide how at so early an age the bright in her eyes was already gone. We two were the only family I could name, and I had no way to know whether it was my mother's doing or not, but I decided that I would not forgive her for making it that way.

I left Momma in the yard and went to my room. I don't know what put the thought in my head, but I knew I wanted to leave. That would take some planning, and money. It was not too long before September, when I would be off to college, but I wanted to go right then. Maybe to Knoxville, maybe to Memphis. Chicago, Kansas City, Boston. I had never been anywhere. I stood in my room for a while, not knowing what to do. I took my fishing tackle from the hall closet and went for the back door. Momma was in the kitchen. She squared her shoulders to say something, but I walked past her for the back door. By the time I realized she was saying, "Don't you slam that screen door in my face," I had already done it. I got in the car and turned it out of the yard. I looked back long enough to see her behind the screen, then I drove off.

I drove to the downtown liquor store, got two bumpers of Colt 45, and buzzed six yellow lights out Valley Road. Once the road passed the Confederate cemetery and crossed Eleventh Street, it was a straight shot until it hit the river. It wound south, along the riverbend and then west, running the length of the valley, bending around the town. It ran a few miles before stretches of solid land gave way to swamp. I drove a ways into the swamp, looking for a place to fish. I pulled off the road, smoked some herb, and carried the malt liquor and my fishing tackle out into the wetlands. There was plenty of nothing out there. Once the road got past the foundry and Donahue's Field, there was nothing but swamp. Small patches of old growth, stands of pine and oak thriving too deep in there for any logging trail or tractor to mess with.

What happened next was simpler than I'd like it to be: I was high, I drank until well after dark, I passed out.

I woke to the whisper Johnson grass made against my leg when I walked through it, but I wasn't the one who was walking. I was doubled over someone's shoulder. The ground was passing below me, grass giving way to work boots. I heard someone say, "You damn lucky your Momma ain't burnt my phone number," and all that I remember after that comes in random flashes: Light of the evening shimmering through the trees before the sky went black. The night air full of wet cold and cicada wail that buzzed inside my skin. Glow of a pitch lantern bobbing above swamp mist. Calvin Powell's wide-boned face, lit by that glow as it drifted through the dark. When Cal carried me out, he knew I'd be embarrassed, so he took me home instead of the hospital. He didn't stop once, but slowed down when I needed to vomit out of the window.

After I had been put to bed, I could hear Momma running dishwater in the empty kitchen sink. Cal's mud-caked boots thudded down the hall and down the stairs. Chairs were dragged from the Florida room to the patio. Momma was still in the kitchen, clinking bottles in the back of the bread drawer, where she kept the bourbon. Sometime in early morning, I woke from some dream I was having about the wet air of high summer, covering me like too many quilts. I stepped to my window to catch the breeze. Cal's truck was still in the driveway, its chalky gray primer coat catching the blue light of the new morning. I woke later to the rumble of Cal's truck pulling out of our drive, and there was Momma, leaning right over me. She was smiling, and I wasn't sure what she was smiling about: Me being safe at home, Cal having been the one to carry me home, or Cal staying through the night.

Momma held my hands tightly in hers so that it would take an effort for me to pull them back. It would have been cruel to do that. But part of me wanted to be hard. I wanted to say something to hurt her, and to say something about earlier that summer, Cal, that swamp, and some woman whose story nobody would ever get right. But Momma kept smiling. How did it work that people could let go of their pasts? Just burn away the parts they didn't want, open their arms to the life they wanted? I wondered what story Momma had made of Glenda and Cal, and what Cal thought of Momma. Burn or bury, forget or not remember: It felt the same. That's when I felt like not remembering would be a good thing for me.

In the days after that—I don't know how many—I kept to my room. I spent most hours waiting for the hounds in my bedroom wallpaper to catch the fox, that or the walleye to escape the hook in the alternating pattern. There was wallpaper watching, reading comic books, and getting up to watch Cal's truck pull into our driveway every evening, watching it rumble out in the early morning.

Momma and I didn't speak much after that. That was fine with me. It was almost fall, and I would be leaving soon. When I started eating supper at the table, those minutes were long, with no talk. Sometimes Momma would say, "Well, Lord knows we got to make do with what we got," and sit staring at the tablecloth with a stillness she reserved for Grace. There would be a silence, and then we would speak of the heat or rain or the collards out back. Then we would be silent, like we had agreed to something.

Before too long I was off to college. We did not speak much while I was away, not until I had graduated and was living back in Watertown. When I was twenty-two, after I'd gone to college, worked some time away and was back home, working small-town insurance claims, Momma had a stroke. She was confined to a wheelchair and couldn't speak. I found a home for her, and a third of my pay went into that. I'd visit her for an hour or so on holidays. Three years of Easter, Thanksgiving, Christmas, and her birthday: me watching her; her looking sometimes at me, sometimes at nothing at all. There were times when her eyes would perk up and she'd open her mouth, as if to ask a question. Or she might reach out her hand toward my sleeve, and sometimes I'd start to lean to her, ready to answer, but I would catch myself. By then she was a woman in a rest home who could not remember that she had been my mother.

The year I turned twenty-five, she passed away in her sleep. I arranged her burial, sold what was left in the house to auctioneers, and moved out of town a few months later.

It hasn't been long since Cherise got out of the car and walked to the bridge, but I'm sure she is tired of waiting for me to say something. From the car I watch her standing on the bridge. The late-day sun is almost full on her face. She looks back for a moment as I open my door, but then quickly returns to her view of the stream. I get out of the car and walk to her. She knows I'm coming, but she's not looking. She's thinking, *no more bullshit.*

I start talking before I get to her. I tell her I couldn't have told her why I had to go back because I wasn't sure myself until I got into Watertown. She looks my way, but doesn't say a word. She leans against the bridge rail. Her arms are folded. I want to hold her while I try to explain, but I know she's not having that.

"No bullshit," I say, and tell her the story about how Calvin Powell, a man with the strength of two, shivered like a child when he whispered Glenda Kendricks's name. I start with that and consider telling her the rest. I pause, not sure of what I'm waiting for.

Cherise listens and asks no questions. I'm thinking that she might ask about family and friends in Watertown, as she did years ago, when she first wondered why I never took her home. I told her then that was my business, and soon we got to talking like folks who were close to last words. Then she got quiet, like now.

She doesn't know the whole of the story, but I can see her working to figure out what I have told her. She thinks she understands what troubles me, and as she considers it she begins to smile. It is not a cruel or cynical smile, but one of pity, as if my story is simply about Cal Powell and Glenda Kendricks. She will be wrong, but she is the sort who is used to figuring things out. She is thinking the reason I came back to Watertown was the same reason I stayed away for all those years, and in a few minutes, she is sure to explain it to me: *Cal Powell represented a confusing part of your childhood—angered youth, small town, no father figure sort of thing—but you didn't want to remember him as a bad man.* If she explains this to me Cherise will look concerned. She will still have that smile that gets me, part sigh, part smirk.

But she says nothing.

I don't know what I will do. Maybe I'll look at her and remember that she's not trying to force me to do anything. I'll take in that face, lit in the haze of the afternoon. I will look away for a moment, see all the miles to drive with this woman and maybe my breath will get short, because I haven't told her everything. I look back to her and though she would hate for me to notice, I'll see some yearning there, too.

Just now, I see Momma's face, caught behind the screen door, its grid making a haze over her features. It is all in flashes now: Momma in that kitchen, the hot day outside of it, the night that followed, the silence that filled the days after that.

Cherise will work on how to feel about Cal, but I'm working out what I have kept to myself: that woman in the kitchen door, her child rushing from the house, and she can't get him to come back. He is gone too quickly, the day too hot and the road too quiet to have words out in the yard; the worn wood of the screen door is swollen with summer heat and catches when she wants it to open. Her arms must have pressed against the screen, her head to the door frame. I see her, still calling after me as she gets that door open. She steps just a few feet into the yard, not to chase, not to explain, but to hope that maybe her boy would come back. Cherise doesn't know this, but she will know the look on my face well enough to take me for real when I say, *I don't know what else to tell you.*

I Got Somebody
in Staunton

for James Farmer

When I walk out of the bathroom these four White boys are staring at me as hard as they did when I first drove into the filling station. But now they're smiling, all four of them, like somebody just told a good joke about the nigger in the toilet. Keri's sitting in my car, laughing with them like they've all known each other since grade school. She probably shined up to them, and they got interested when she said something like *my name's Keri, with an "i,"* and ran her hands through her hair, the same way she warmed on to me just two hours ago.

All of them look tired. They have long, washed-out faces, like each of them has done time—maybe the overnight lockup more than once, father with a bottle, lover with a fist, working too many months on third shift, weeks of pork fat and cabbage, too many years stuck in nowhere with nobody to blame for it. Right then, because she's in the middle of these squint-eyed men, because her skin looks more like theirs than mine, because they are all smiling, I get the feeling like running is a good thing to do. My Uncle Izelle used to say when the time comes, running takes you over before you know it's an answer. More than once he'd tell me *don't wait on the answer.*

It's moments like this when I know I have to think fast, but I get caught in all the choices: What's bound to happen? Which move should I make or miss? Time slips on me, I get caught in the heat and haze of the day, and here comes Uncle Ize's voice, buzzing my head with every bit of advice I never wanted: I'm back to fifteen years old, sitting in Ize's car, parked a quarter mile into a field. The sun has just dipped past the tree line, and the air is thick with pollen haze and fireflies, rising from the hay. Ize sips on some corn, looks straight ahead. He talks to the grass, but speaks to me. *Some folks, Clive, you got to step past. Walk on. Some folks don't got a mind for that. The Scottsboro Boys, they was out of work, but lookin'. They was runnin' the freights, always mixin' it up with White folks who was doin' the same. Happy go lucky they was till them boys got to trading blows with the wrong White folks at the wrong time. Next thing, they in the lockup, waitin' on the hangman. All that 'cause a White girl was in the mix. You get near mess like that, walk before you cain't.* He would get to talking like that without any prompt, from out of the blue, it seemed, no event to relate, no reason for why I should remember it, no beginning to the story, no end. There were dozens of drives down country roads, all of them moments I didn't recognize then as lessons until moments like now.

Then my eyes catch the sun. I look to the ground. I refocus, raise my head. I'm looking at the car, the men, and Keri. I'm back to feeling like a twenty-eight-year-old history professor, stuck in another situation where graduate degrees, pedagogical discourse, and academic distinction don't mean shit. I walk along the storefront, feel the change in my pocket. I'm thinking of Bayard Rustin, snuck out of Montgomery in the trunk of a car. When I get to the Coke machine, I stare right back at the four of them. Here I am out in the sticks again, this close to losing my Black ass, and all I can do is hope that when I put the quarters in the slot, the Coke will pull smoothly from the machine, it will be cold, I'll sip it without spilling as I walk around the back of the car, the engine will start when the key turns, and they will move when I step on the gas.

They keep smiling, like that joke is still good and it must be damn funny, gets better by the moment, because they know I have to walk past them to get in the car. It's Uncle Izelle's car, the Impala he bought when he made foreman; master carpenter eighteen years before they gave him the nod. Eighteen years of Jim Crow cracking his back for that car. He built a garage for it: cinderblock with cedar tongue-and-groove paneling outside, ceramic glaze tiles inside. He painted the car once but stuck with the same sapphire blue finish. It still gets waxed twice a month. Two of them are sitting on the hood, the other two stand at the fender. Keri just sits there, grinning in the passenger seat.

And this is where running doesn't make sense. It's my damn car, Uncle Ize's Impala. I had paid my gas, been courteous, even thrown in the two-dollar tip on a top-off. The station worker has already rolled back under a Nova in the garage, but these four hang around like they own the place. I'm sure they think they do. When I first pulled in, they got up from their bench to check me out: brother driving a convertible with a blond-haired girl in the passenger seat. And there were the four of them, not working at the station, but eyeing me like it was a job. They glared like I forgot some rule. But until I end up shot, hung, or beat up in the backseat of a police car, I'm going to drive where I want to, stop where I want to, ride in my car who I want to. Besides, any fool knows no man needs to run from a situation when driving away will do just as good.

I turn my back to the car, watch them in the narrow reflection of the Coke machine's door. I take my time, like picking a Coke takes work. They turn back to her, and she rests her foot up on the dash. Just before I open the door to pull out my bottle, one of them leans in close, laying his best line on her. I can't hear it, but he's trying to be smooth; he eases his hip into the doorframe, a hand on the open door, the other hangs from a thumb in the belt loops of low-slung jeans. He's almost grabbing his crotch, like he must have seen on some play-gangsta rap video. She laughs up to the sky and pulls the car door shut with her heel. He cusses, faking like his hand is hurt, but for just a moment he cups his crotch like he knows what almost got caught. He's the only one who isn't laughing.

One of them says, "Good thing you a quick 'un, Jackie, else you might be grabbin' your fam'ly," and punches Jackie in the arm.

In the thin reflection of glass I can see only one of them now, and soon he steps out of view. I can see the car and I can see her in it, smacking her gum, pushing her cuticles back. She smiles to herself, maybe because she just put the shake on four guys at once, maybe because the radio's tuned to a good song—even though I told her to turn it off when we stopped—or maybe because she knows she's playing me for farther down the road than they could take her. Whatever it's about, she's smiling. She lounges like someone who never had to worry over making time to lounge.

When I met her two hours ago in Fredericksburg she was eased across two barstools. I wasn't at the bar five minutes before she started smiling at me. She kept brushing her elbow next to mine, staring at how, for all of the suntanning she must have done, my arm was a deeper brown than hers. She looked around at the other men in the bar, dark on the arms from day labor, but still paler than me. *You've never been in this bar either,* that's what she said first. This had her laughing: me, bumping through the door in the early afternoon, eyes red from too much heat and no water, and not clear headed enough to notice that it wasn't a bar where brothers hung out. But once I was ten feet into the place, I figured I had a right to have one beer wherever I wanted. I had sat down at the empty end of the bar, waited a while to get served. I got my beer and stared at the reworking of Mount Rushmore painted on the brick wall: Jeff Davis, Robert E. Lee, Jeb Stuart, and Stonewall Jackson. I didn't have two pulls off the bottle before this girl was edging her elbow next to mine. She wouldn't stop smiling: *what you doing in here?*

I couldn't say much to that. I don't know what got me into that bar on that afternoon. I was headed to Staunton again, to visit Uncle Ize, who was dying. Sometimes I'd have a few drinks in some bar in Fredericksburg—always a different bar, I don't know why—get a little buzz on to speed up that same trip I'd been taking for three months now. Once a week along the byways: from Fredericksburg, through Gordonsville and Orange, past Cismont and Charlottesville, over Afton Mountain and just south of Staunton, to a small driveway running switchbacks up a hill, where Uncle Izelle lay in the house he built thirty years back.

Except for his bedroom, the rooms of Izelle's house were empty, stale with thirty years of Pall Mall smoke and Ize's tarlung hack. Most of the furniture was gone. He couldn't make his way into the other rooms, and because he couldn't see to dying as quickly as the family expected, the relatives had started clearing the house to pay the bills. The living room suite to buy a hospital bed; Auntie Dora's china sold for his intubator, couch and dining room table for Meals on Wheels. His room was now his home: newspapers pushed to the corners; pictures of cars and trucks he had owned; yellowed clippings of Bob Gibson, Hank Aaron, Oscar Robertson; Count Basie and Jimmy Rushing records; four-poster bed with quilts Aunt Dora had made; five-gallon water dispenser; side table for pills and muscle rub; laundry rack—one towel, two washcloths, handkerchief, boxers, socks, pajamas; trousers, shirts, ties, and suits were in a box, bound for the clothing drive the Shrine put on every winter. After a while the house looked less like a home, so folks stopped treating it like one. When my cousin Pearline called to say that they had forgotten him to soil his own bed, I started making my drive to Staunton.

Once a week I would leave after teaching Friday's last class and make the two-hour drive to sit with Uncle Izelle. After a few visits, he started to fuss about my taking too long to get there, even though we had never set a time for me to arrive. He grew used to seeing me, so already had in his mind when he wanted me there. My truck didn't move fast enough for him. One day I walked into his room, and he was lying there with his fist balled on his chest. He said, *get here sooner*, and he opened his fingers to give me the keys to his car.

I wore a groove into the wicker of his bedside rocker that summer. I would bring the *Post*, old copies of *Ringside* and *Jet* magazines from the barbershop in Fredericksburg. In the late light of the day, when the shade was on the bedroom side of the house, I'd open the window and turn off the air conditioner, let the smell of cut hay and black locust drift into the room as Ize dozed off. I would read for an hour. I don't know if I was reading for him or me. All I know is that sometimes, when I stopped mid-sentence to watch his face ease into sleep, I would relax, too. I'd forget about bills and committee meetings, stacks of papers waiting for me to grade. I would look out the window, across the heat working witchwater over the fields, out to the Blue Ridge and think, *it don't make no damn difference what day it is, how hot it is or isn't, how fast or slow I get here, or how many times I'll be back, all that matters is that I'm here.*

I told Keri all of this over a second drink, and she just smiled. She let me talk through my drinks, nodded at the right lines, laughed at what she thought I tried to make funny. She knew when to be polite. She was good at making talk out of quiet. We talked for a half hour or so while I drank. It doesn't take that long for two drinks, but when she kept talking to me and nobody around seemed bothered about it, I milked those beers. I don't know why. *That's what get you hung*, Ize would say.

When she found out where I was headed, she said, *I got somebody in Staunton.* And I said, *Who's that?* She smiled and ran her hair behind her ear. *You*, she said. I laughed at that: *How you think that up, since we just meetin'?* She kept moving her hair behind her ears, like she thought that was attractive. I wanted to laugh at that, too. *For a teacher, you don't speak all that well,* she said. *I'm a professor,* I said, *and when I'se pro-fessin' I's natchul good at speechifyin'.* That was my job during the week. But right then, I was going to see Izelle, my people. When we got together, I told her, we didn't *speak so good,* but the talk was clear. She left that alone and got back to working on that ride.

She said, *by the time you give me a ride, I'll know somebody in Staunton.* She had a mouthful of white teeth. One in the front of her bottom row was chipped. When she wasn't messing with her hair, she tapped a fingernail against that tooth. She smiled and brushed a lock from her eyes. She was headed for Staunton, at least that far, and it didn't make her no never mind how she got there.

How do you figure, just like that, we gonna be friends, I said, *just because I'm thinking about carrying you down the road?* I'm not the flirting type, but I hadn't left the bar, either. I could see Ize looking at me from way back in my childhood: We would be on the porch, some farmer's daughter would drive by in her daddy's truck, hair blowing like a Breck girl's out the window when her daddy would rather her keep it in a bun. I'd be staring, less at the girl and more at that hair; it looked like everything I saw on TV. I never saw any afros in the Ford and Miller High Life ads, in the Saturday movie, on the news or game shows. I used to wonder why this was: Was the 'fro too big for tight camera shots, maybe it muffled actors' lines, all that Afro Sheen, bound to take flame under set lights. But every show was full of country-girl hair, red, blond, and brunette "because-I'm-worth-it" sort of hair. I'd be caught up in all of that and turn to see if Uncle Ize was seeing what I was seeing, but he'd be looking dead at me: *Emmett Till was a happy boy, a bit on the plump side, big-tooth smile. Boy walked around with a tilt to his cap, tossed a care like a tissue. Look too at a White lady one day and woke up dead in a river, face shot off, mill fan tied around his neck.* Then he'd turn back to looking at the fields, and the rest of our day would be quiet.

Keri sat next to me at that bar, the both of us silent for a while. Then she ordered another round. When the drinks came she said, *well, sometimes you never know just who is gonna get you to the place you need to be.* And I was trying to make sense of what the hell she meant by that when she downed half her bourbon. *Maybe this ride is gonna be special,* she said. She fanned the heat from her halter top with the shirt she wore over it—a man's shirt, with tight stripes and holes for cufflinks. She flapped that shirt like she might take it off, but when the men down the bar took notice, she tied it at her waist and bumped at my elbow again. I think she knew I was going to give her a ride, even if I couldn't reason why.

From the start, I saw through her toe rings and messy amber blonde hair, four or five bunches winding into dreadlocks. She said she was living in Dunwoody—she wouldn't say Richmond proper—but I figured her for a woman trying to hide a golf club and Monument Avenue past. She reminded me of students I taught: teens driving SUVs to Dave Matthews Band concerts, flashing daddy's gold card to get back at the old man for giving them money without attention. When I sprung that idea on her she said, *you be nice, life ain't been no crystal stair for me, neither,* and there was some sass to her voice, like she had

55

practiced in the mirror some blend of Maya Angelou and Flip Wilson from his Geraldine days. She knew how to wave her finger, shift her weight from hip to hip, suck at her teeth. That's when I guessed that sometime—eight months or so earlier—she had started twisting her hair into locks. Before I could say a word, she told me her hair was *kinky* because there was some *ethnic folks* in her, somewhere, *some kinda way* down the line. She was working gum between her front teeth, smacking it like a hairdresser. Drinking beer, and still she was smacking that gum, doing it to show out, like my Auntie Pearline does when somebody works her last nerve. *You got that soul-sistah thing down,* I had to laugh at her for that, *how many Aretha albums you got?*

She got hot at that. *How do you know we're not related,* she said, *not directly, you know, but skin alone ain't all of it.* She was letting me know she had it down. I was the only brother in the bar and she was getting loud with me, calling me out so others heard it, but she was smiling. She kept on smiling; that's how I was supposed to know I could ease up to her.

I looked past her shoulder to the men along the bar, looking back at me and the noise she was making. *What the hell you doing in my bar,* that's what was in their eyes, and I knew if she was going to ride with me, we'd have to get going soon. I stared back at those men and I was thinking that before we left, I would have to tell her, *you think hard on one thing: it's my car getting you where you got to go,* but I held back. It was only a trip down Route 20 south that she needed—Fredericksburg to Staunton—and that was on my way. I was looking at her ass as we walked out of the door, and Ize's voice rang in my head again: *Remember what happened to Tom Robinson. Just for*

steppin' in that lady's yard. Don't matter he was helpin' her to bust
that chiffarobe or anything else. They shot his ass like it was good-
payin' work. You the professor, son, but that ain't just some wrote-
down story.

I open the machine door to get my Coke. All that's left is Nehi
grape. I turn to face the car and I'm almost back to feeling
calm. The Impala shimmers in the sun, and past it, those four
dirty-blond suckers shuffle down the road, their shoulders all
sloped the same, BVDs riding above their buttless jeans, each
trying not to look too eager about following the others back to
whatever boredom must be waiting. One looks back at me,
and his face is twisted in a frown, like it's my fault, whatever
no-job, rust-out-trailer-and-crabgrass-yard world is waiting
for him down that road.

When I turn back to the car, she's smiling at me, like the
joke she never told is still in her mind, and when I get to the
car, she will tell it. I take my time. Put the bottle to my head,
let the cool sink in. Turn back to the machine, pop the cap off.
Take a slow sip. Wash that cold sip around in my mouth until
it's warm and thick and tastes sweet enough to spit out. I
think about doing just that, to see what she does.

I walk back to the car. She's rubbing lotion into her shoulders. She's saying "Fredericksburg, Wilderness, Orange, Gordonsville, Cismont, Charlottesville, Esmont," for no reason.
I'm thinking maybe that's the punchline to the joke.

"Maybe I let you off in Orange," I tell her.

Her smile gets slim, but she says, "What's the matter? Your
car don't know the way to Staunton?"

"I know Staunton, but I'm not sure about you and me and the car making Staunton at the same time."

"That's gonna be unfortunate for one of us," she says, and starts to play with her hair.

"Since I'm driving and you riding, who you figure that will be?"

"Could be anybody."

A half hour later we are passing farmland south of Wilderness, hills rolling to the Blue Ridge, houses and outbuildings the same worn-out gray as fieldstones too big to move. She's singing "Travlin' Light."

I haven't heard that in a long while. "I love Billie Holiday," I say.

"That's a Chet Baker song," she says.

"Did he sing 'Strange Fruit,' too?"

"Do what?"

And I let that one go.

She smiles, happy with herself. She stretches out, dangles a foot over the door.

"That scene back there," I said. "Don't pull no more shit like that."

"The filling station? Those boys were just trying to fool around with something they don't know nothing about. You're not upset about that, are you?"

I stay quiet, thinking that she will figure it out.

"You have got to ease up." She's humming again. "This is Louisa County: just Range Rovers and show horses."

"I don't roll so easy through here."

"What's going to happen?"

"If you got to ask that, you missed some history."

"Those boys was just having fun."

"I'll remember that in Orange."

"You got to ease up, Cliff. 'Virginia is for Lovers.' "

"Clive."

"What?"

"Name's Clive."

"Oh, I know, but ease up," she said, "To *clive*, to *cliff*, will *clive*, will *cliff*, to have *clived*, to have—Cliff fits best."

"Not in my car it don't."

She doesn't say anything for a while after that. That feels fine to me. The quiet suits me better. Sometimes when it's hot out, I turn off the radio and listen to the drone of the tires on the road. The summer haze has its own quiet buzz. Trees rush past in a blur. Boxwoods edging horse farms. Sycamore running the bottoms. Tulip poplar along roadside. As the car passes them, all you know is a pocket of quick silence, a hush that's there and then isn't. Every few miles a white oak arches over the road, and when you drive under, the air above is quiet just long enough to notice the drone of the fields—dogs barking where you can't see, tractors rumbling the back acres, chatter of grackles on the power lines—and you almost forget where you are or where you're going.

One summer, years back, I was down into Charlottesville every weekend for six weeks to see Uncle Ize, laid up in the university hospital with one lung gone black and an oxygen tube up his nose for good. I came to know that hour-and-twenty-minute drive as the only time during the whole week I could not remember. I can't say if the hay was high or already disced for winter. How many times did I stop at or run the flashing red light where Route 20 crosses 522? One afternoon

I saw a field on fire; it burned hot and fast like pine shavings, but I can't recall if it was midsummer or late.

I'm thinking on that when we pass farmhouses outside Gordonsville. There's no sound but the rush of heat over the windshield of the car. We are almost to the junction for the road to Culpepper, and up ahead there's a line of cars at the town rotary. An old International Harvester flatbed loaded with hay discs is rolling slowly at the front of the line. The truck takes too sharp a turn through the rotary and crosses the center line a couple of times before settling into the right lane of the byway stretching straight out of town—young truck driver learning to coax a tricky clutch. He's having trouble, and we're stuck at the end of the line of cars his trouble is making. As soon as we drive slowly past the town marker, the fields open up again. Young corn and collards run the furrows over low hills. I ease back, my hand on the dash above the radio, and turn to her, sitting with her knees to her chest, sulking.

She wants the music back on. I had turned it off when we left Wilderness. She had some music on, something loud, and I turned it off. I put up my hand, above the windshield, into the oncoming air and let it blow the sweat from my palm. Then I brought my hand down, to just above her knees and gestured to the row of tulip poplar we were passing. *Listen,* I said and I put my hand on the dash above the radio. Poplar petals blew by like flax and buzzed as they brushed over the windsheild. There was quiet for ten more trees and then the open-air hush of the fields.

She was looking at me, smiling, not caring, waiting for the music, knowing that it was my damn car and it would be silent for a while. She was going along with it until we got caught in the line behind the truck.

Finally she says, "now that we've been nature lovin' for a while, you mind if I change up the mood?" She laughs and puts her feet on the dash.

I look at her, smiling, out of her sulk, rubbing lotion into her shins.

"Listen," she giggles, bugging her eyes, *"listen."*

I take my hand from the dash, and she says, "I knew he was a music lover." She waits until we pick up speed before she turns the radio back on. She works it slowly, with the volume down low, and when she finds the station she wants she says, "Oh, this is my *song,*" and turns it up—some band trying to sound like the Rolling Stones trying to sound like Muddy Waters. By the time the Harvester finds high gear, we are going fast again and the music is part of the hot air rushing past.

Uncle Ize was careful about who rode in his car. If he was in his truck, he'd pick up as many strangers as would fit in the bed and cab, but not just anybody got in the Impala. No pets. No kids. Few women. *Too much trouble,* he used to say, *always busy with the lighter and the radio; and you got to keep the top up, else they hair gets worked over, messing with my rearview to check for lipstick on they teeth—you know it's a damn mirror under the sun flap.* But for years before his wife died, Aunt Dora was the only person other than him in that car on a Saturday. I'd be mowing the yard or raking cuttings, and that Impala would come breezing down the road, Ize and Dora dressed for a cookout or a party. When he wasn't riding her around he passed his time in that car. He'd say he was going fishing, but he never came back with fish. He wasn't a church-going man, but he took Sunday drives—leisure suit, cigarillos, straw porkpie, Billy Eckstine on the stereo. *Why buy a car I ain't gonna drive?* he used to say when folks got to teasing him about being in that car more than his house. *Cousin, I ain't the man to lay up in the house all day.*

When I got to be thirteen or so, he would pull into our yard on a Saturday, watch me sweat over that rake for a while. I'd try not to look at that car too long, sun gleaming across the chrome and into the iridescent finish like the light was coming from the car. *Let's us go ridin'*, he'd say, and I'd step inside to change my clothes. We rode the byways. Over Afton Mountain, around Charlottesville, along Skyline Drive, down quiet wooded roads. I'd know we reached where he wanted to go when he turned off the radio. Sometimes we were near water, but never a fishing hole.

On the first trip, he eased the car along a tractor lane until we reached a two-hundred-year-old black oak in the middle of an abandoned hayfield. He pulled under the shade of the tree, carried a cigarillo and his flask to the knuckle of a root, and sat down. *Look around, get a feel for the place,* he said and pointed up into the boughs. *Listen.* I could hear crows fussing in the birches at the edge of the field. Chickadees and wrens buzzed the hay. When I looked up, there was wind, a slight whisper in the leaves, but other than that I heard nothing. The air felt still and close. I wanted to hear something but I didn't know what I was listening for. I walked around the tree, spiraling out until I was in sun, away from where the shade felt like a room with no windows. Ize sipped at his flask, and chewed on that cigarillo. After a while he got up, lit his smoke, and said, *let's go.* I thought we'd listen to Eckstine and Basie on the way back, but he was silent all the way to my yard, even after I got out, and he backed the car out of the driveway.

Next month, we pulled up to the bluffs above a quarry. The mountain silverbells there had trunks thick as culvert drain pipes and their boughs angled far over the bluff. We watched the sun drop until it lit the underside of the leaves. Ize shared his cucumber sandwich, and we rode home not too long after dark.

Two weeks later he drove me to a coal silo rising from a blanket of honeysuckle and kudzu. A supply shed, the spine of old railway, and three rotting boxcars were nothing more than soft rises in a world of vines. In a month, kudzu would cover the silo, too. We stood in the circle of shade and exposed gravel underneath. Steel braces ran from the stone base to the belly of the silo. Ize stepped from under the silo but motioned for me to stay where I was. He pointed up to where the steel beams angled into darkness of the burnt-out silo. *Nobody remembers this one,* he said.

The month after that, he told me *listen* as we rolled through stands of loblolly and white pine. *What you got out here?* I laughed. It had been a good ride: He had let me drive for a few miles. We ate the pulled pork Dora had packed with biscuits in his lunch pail. This was another of Izelle's mystery rides, but I thought this was some grown-up version of the "I Spy" game I used to play in the backseat with my sister. I was sure that on one of these trips he was going to show me some secret only a teenage boy would appreciate: a hole to hide money, spots to sneak drinks with the boys, a place to take a girl. But he pulled a wad of paper out of his pocket: a wallet-size set of folded photos, bound with a rubber band. They were old photos and postcards, faded, distorted by age and creases, but when he put them in my hand, I knew what they were. *You look here, Clive,* Ize said, *this from nineteen-nineteen, outside Roanoke. Daddy give me this; kep' it in his billfold. That's the trestle running the train into Richmond. Boy was strung from that bridge and left for a week, wasn't noboby allowed to cut him down. See on the bank? A mess of crackers, thick like it's the State Fair. Look at their faces. They lovin' it. 'Cause they got them one. They look like they havin' a big time, but I tell you this: they afraid. They don't study it too much, but they afraid, like that boy's a dog you got to watch and whup. You remember that. Nineteen-nineteen. They lynched over six hundred that summer.* He didn't say much more after that. He would unfold one, look at it like it was new, and then hand it to me. Together we looked through the rest: A boy hanged from an oak tree; open-casket photo of Emmett Till, his face bloated and sewn together; the torsos of two men on a post, their legs burnt into the ashes around them; a man hanged from a river derrick, face caved in, blood running from the mangled flesh that once made him a man.

When my mind leaves that day in the pines, I'm back in the car, speeding a straight stretch, and it takes me a moment to remember that Keri's sitting next to me.

Ahead, an explosion of hay spills into a bend in the road. By the time I slow into the turn, the road is covered with straw, the cars kicking up wakes of hay. Just in front, skid marks lead to three cars jammed together, halfway onto the shoulder. Ahead of them, a Dodge is buried in hay, its front end tucked into the underside of the Harvester, which lies on its side across the road. By the time I pull up behind the tenth

car back, a man from the fifth truck is already walking our
way. He turns the bill of his cap from back to front, cups it to
cover his eyes from the setting sun. The beginning of what
looks like his first beard sprouts from his cheeks. He smacks
his hands against his jeans, wipes them on his chest. His shirt
reads, *If I Can't Live Without Her, Why Ain't I Dead?*

"We ain't going nowhere, no time soon," he says without
breaking stride, "want something from the store?"

"Rolling papers," Keri says.

"Party, party," he says without missing a step.

I'm still caught up in wondering what I wanted—water,
beer, nothing—when I hear what Keri's said. Whatever's going to happen is already in motion. I watch him walk down
the line of cars to a store a half mile back. The sun is just past
his shoulders. Someone has written *Timmy* with a marker on
the back of his shirt.

Keri stands up, drops down, gets out of the car. "Party,
party," she whispers, rummages through her bag, looks to the
fields on either side of us. She scans the hills and bottoms, outbuildings and tree lines. She spins to take in the land and turns
again, slower and slower, like she'll choose the spot where the
bottle in her head points when it stops spinning. Her hands
hold a banana-size bag of weed against her belly. She points to
a spot under a sycamore. The tree bends out over a small pond
and a bank of red mud where cattle take their drink. "I didn't
bring enough for everyone," she says. Her voice fades to a
whisper again when she says, "Let's move off the road."

I ease the Impala off the road and I'm thinking, *you got-
damn right we gonna move off the road.* How would I explain it?
Me, Keri, and *Timmy* stuck in a line of cars on a Virginia by-

way, puffing on jays. That's when a trooper rolls up; when a colleague looks out of her rearview; when anybody from between Fredericksburg and Staunton who knows my family cruises by.

I'm thinking that I should head straight for Orange, drop Keri off to do what she pleases. I can imagine her surprise when I tell her this. It's a face I've seen before, the face many of my students have when my version of history doesn't match theirs. I'm preparing the lecture I'll give Keri, when I get to thinking about Ize. A couple of years back I was living with Uncle Ize and Auntie Dora while I finished off my dissertation. I started sneaking out after the first month I moved in. There was no reason for it, not as far as I could explain, but if somebody asked me about it then, I might have said that I was being respectful to Ize and Dora. I didn't have a car, but I wanted to get a drunk on every now and then to cut the tedium of days at the computer. I'd meet up with high school friends and folks who never went to school, folks I'd meet over a cooler of beer in some field or by a river. I got into a little groove: eat supper, play whist or dominoes with Ize and Dora, watch the ball game, make like I was turning in to read, and go out the back window an hour after Ize cut off the porch lights. I thought I was slick for a month of Fridays, until one Saturday morning, when I was riding with Ize to the hardware store, he pulled the truck down a gravel road. It was early morning. I was hung over. *Eddie Jenks said he saw you stumbling the road last night, kneewalking like a drunk schoolboy.* He stared at me a while. Then he took a piece of paper out of his wallet. *You grown and you supposed to be smart, but you could learn a thing or two from this old nigger.* The paper was less wrinkled than others he'd shared with me. It was a newspaper clipping about James Byrd, murdered in Texas. *You look at this.* Ize held onto it for a moment before he let me take it. *Brother just walkin' a country lane, met up with some good ole boys on the side of the road. He's thinkin' he's gettin' a ride into town, see his lady, have him a drank. They stood that boy behind a truck, chained him to the bumper, sped up while he ran to keep up. They kep' on like that, till he couldn't stay on his feet, an' then they kep' on. Time they had they fun, half the man's body was all over Texas; head and arm tore clean off. This wasn't no Jim Crow years, professor. This was nineteen ninety-nine, last year, hear me? When they sentence the cracker what done it, he comin' out the courthouse and when they ask what all he got to say to the dead boy's momma, all he could say was "fuck you."*

I'm thinking on Ize, waiting for me in Staunton with his fists balled on his chest. I'm about to turn the car back onto the road when Keri puts her hand on my arm.

"Wait. Here comes Timmy."

Timmy comes up with a box of fried chicken, a twelve-pack of beer, and a pack of ZigZags tucked under the strap of his baseball cap. As he passes by, he flips the rolling papers to Keri. "I'd give you a beer but that might make us more friendly than we had in mind," he says to Keri and heads for his truck. When he's past the car, Keri bucks her pelvis and mouths *party, party* to his back.

Keri already has a joint lit by the time I stop the car under the sycamore in the field. She takes her toke and turns off the radio after she passes it to me. I hit the jay, pass it back. Just past the hood of the car, the sun is low on the Blue Ridge. The first treefrogs of the evening call from the bottoms. The sky turns violet above the canopy of the tree.

Keri takes another hit, passes it to me, and puts her feet across my lap. She relaxes her neck and tilts her head back.

"You know what's funny?" She laughs her smoke up into the tree. "Those boys at the filling station, they were excited to meet you."

"I bet they was."

"I told them you were Michael Jordan's brother."

"That's a lie."

"No, I did. Just to see what they would do."

"What'd they do?"

"Not much. Stood there, smiling at each other, like idiots. They wanted to meet you, but I said you were on a private vacation."

"I was?"

"You didn't want to be bothered with fans. That's when they got pouty."

I look out to the light dimming over the field. All I can think to say is "Ain't that some shit?"

"I don't even like Michael Jordan," she says and nudges a toe against my ribs. For a moment she looks older than what I'd guessed her to be. Her face eases from a smile to a smirk. I'm not sure which part of her joke she means as funny. I take in the herb, let it out, watch her features go soft. When the last of the sun catches her hair, her face is glowing.

I lean to pass her the joint and I see Timmy's truck pull up to a cattle run about fifty yards between the pond and the road. Timmy's in the back. He hops out, throws a bottle, walks a ways into the field, and unzips to piss. Another guy—baseball cap, T-shirt, dirty jeans—gets out of the cab with the beer. He sits on the tailgate as Timmy walks back to the truck. The other guy points our way as he hands Timmy another beer. Timmy turns, stoops to look, waves at us.

Keri waves back.

"You want some cocktails?" he yells across the field.

Keri jumps out of the car and starts his way. I ease back into my seat, check out Timmy's truck: rust and royal blue, fishing rod and baseball bat in the gun rack, wood-plank bumper where the chrome used to be. I look to see how far we are from the road. After a few minutes, I follow her across the field.

When I get there, Keri's already sipping on a beer. Timmy is hitting the joint while a man who looks like Timmy's brother—older or younger, I can't tell—watches him hold his smoke.

"This is Al." Timmy exhales. Al grins like a fifth grader who's just farted. "He calls me Timmy. Want some Miller Hi-Life?"

"You're a good man, Timmy." I say and drink half the beer in one draw.

By the time we've all had two, the sun has set and fireflies begin to flash all over the fields. When it's dark, their lights make a lake of green glitter clear to the tree line.

Timmy finishes his third, knocks Al's hat off, and says, "Let's us shoot some bottles." He pulls a rifle from under the toolbox in the truck bed. Al flicks the truck's headlights to light up the cattle run. Timmy lines up our bottles along the top beam. He opens another beer and begins looking for bullets in the toolbox.

Timmy wheels the rifle my way. "Only got one gun. You can go next."

I pour out the rest of my beer and put it on the beam. As I walk out of the headlights, I keep walking into the field.

"Where you going?" Keri calls after me.

"Just walking for a while," I say, turning to face her. I can only see her silhouette. "I used to live on the edge of a field where every summer the fireflies were just like this. I'd go into the middle of the field, sit still, and watch them rise from the hay. It's something to see." And I turn to walk into the fireflies, drifting through the dark.

"You're making that up." She laughs.

"Too good to be true," I say. "I'm going to take a piss."

"I'll be out there in a minute to check on you."

I walk into the field. Around me, the green sparks of fireflies shine everywhere but a ten-foot ring of dark around me. They keep their distance as I walk into them. As I move, the dark circle moves with me. I turn back when I've walked about hundred yards away. I can see her in the glare of Timmy's trucklights. She's bent over in laughter. She straightens up and walks out of the light, her silhouette drifting in the same direction she saw me walk. I shift out of the line of her path, crouch in the hay, and watch her walk past. Timmy and Al start firing at the bottles, sharp flashes of light and then a report that echoes past me and into the trees. Keri jumps and turns back to see Al shoot a bottle. She runs toward the truck. When she gets there she pulls out her bag of weed. As she turns her back to roll a joint, I make my way to the Impala. I figure that even if she hears the car pull out or sees me pull off, she won't be that bothered. One of those boys is sure to get her where she wants to go.

I back the car away from the pond with my lights off. When all four wheels are on the pavement, I turn on the lights. I drive off, slow down 20 south, and then fast, hard on the curves. Ize will be awake, waiting on me. He doesn't need to know who I was riding in his car. I figure I can run the Impala through an auto wash so that even though he couldn't see it, Ize would know his car was looking good when he heard me pulling it into his garage.

Urban Renewal

for my mother, Jo Katherine, who got me this far

I seen it as a sign. Over there, on Hartford Street, the Black
House was gone. Just a hole in the ground. It wasn't but a day
after Donnell was shot and I was coming from work. Folks living or dying, bills don't wait for you to catch up, and it was
better to be busy with something. Answering 411 calls got me
working on somebody else's problem. You know: *Who are you
looking for? What street? I got five Salazars on Broad Avenue, three
in the same building. Which do you want first?* But it was one of
those next-to-my-last-nerve days, and I wasn't waiting in the
cold on no bus to carry me the long way around the College
property, so I made a shortcut across the ball fields. That's
when I saw the House was missing and figured there wasn't no
easy answer to that hole.

We had a late-winter snow and wasn't nobody out there,
not even kids from the neighborhood, who play ball out there
until they get run off by the College police. As I walked across
the ball fields, I looked through the iron fence that surrounded
the College. The College land cut straight through my neighborhood. There was a fence, old-style pointy-top iron bars,

around the whole place. If there wasn't a fence, I would be real close to home. I lived across the street. But the gate was near the edge of the College's land, a ways farther, even with my shortcut. I could see through the fence to the red mud of the empty lots across the street from the College. Red lots next to my house, too, where there used to be folks' houses before the College bought them and tore them down. It was a lot of land to see so bare.

Donnell used to tell me, *Momma, the College police is hard on townfolk*. And even though he was young, he would know about those police, because more than once he come home, sweat from nappy head to ashy knees, running all the way from the College with stories about nightsticks and big flashlights and how they almost run him down in the street. A couple of times they call me over there to carry him home after they catch him riding his bike on the campus. Donnell didn't start trouble. That boy was raised up *right*: Police or no police, he didn't step out of line because he knew I would hear about it. And Momma was worse than any police. My boy was raised right.

But there wasn't a safe place for riding bikes around our way—too many cars racing between blocks—so the kids would ride over to the College. It's like a park up in there, tall trees in rows, pathways, gardens, and fountains. They got a big machine there, a vacuum on a truck, that drives around that place once a week sucking up leaves. Not a leaf in sight. Come fall, the trees look like October and the grass looks like July. Money made all of that work. And they got nervous when city-folk was around all that.

That College was smack in the middle of our neighborhood; not a soul over there come from 'round my way, but they was there, running things, talking in the papers about urban renewal, city planning, community outreach—words rich folks throw around when they buy land near poor folks. But that place is like a fortress. That old-style ironwork fence used to have working gates when I was a girl. After a while they kept the fence up and took the gates down, so it look like anybody could walk right through there. But they was still worried over their kids being safe. They hired more police, put up a fence across Hartford Street, so can't nobody drive through there. Hartford Street was a *public* street. The quickest way across town, and the College got the City to close it up. That's money. So when he told me years ago about how they treat you over at the College, I figured Donnell would know, even if he was just a boy then.

That was back in those tightfisted Reagan years, when wasn't nobody with long money thinking much about anybody who was making getting-by money. But they was afraid of us all the same. They say it's different now, but White kids with *Free Tibet!* bumper stickers still lock their car doors when they ride down my street. In '85, Donnell was eleven and getting around like any boy, riding that bike all over and back. The College police was steady on him like he's doing something wrong. He was riding a bike. The College is always in the news, talking about *working with community,* but after the way they got so worked up about Donnell rolling through there, it was hard to talk to him about any kind of college. He was always college smart, but he was real young when he figured he wasn't going to get into that mess if folks at a college treated him like they did. After a while none of us went up through the College much anymore.

But a day after my boy was dead and gone, I wasn't bothered with no police or nobody else's worried mind, because it was cold, and it smelled like rain more than snow, and the last of the leaves was off the branches and sharp on my face, and because before Donnell was old enough to sit on a bike seat, I already worked cleaning up dormitory mess after them College kids for close to ten years, so I figure I had my right to walk through there.

I cut across the ball fields, thinking how I'll talk to all the folks calling to say they sorry about Donnell. I was at the end of the field, coming up to Hartford Street. The bus ran down there before the College closed the street off; somebody's child got roughed up and they figured neighborhood types up and down Hartford was nothing they wanted a part of, so they closed it off. I was going down Hartford, get some goat curry at Ervin's Snak-In, right on the corner, and get on home.

Usually I made my turn right where the fields ended, across the street from the Black House. It was a big place, as big as the house I lived in with five other apartments in it. I don't know who all lived there, but I'd see those kids carrying their books in and out of that house, across that campus, and that was a prideful thing for me, even if that wasn't where Donnell found his way. It was good to see them walking in and out of a big house, through the *front* door, no deliveries, no yard work, just living and eating there, because that was the natural thing for them. The house was Victorian, and my sister Janeece like to laugh when I'd say that, *Vic-torian,* like I was somebody bigger than I was, but I told her, *I read the paper, I read books. Black folks can know things, too.* But she just laughs on where all that is gonna get me.

The College called it the Akwaaba House. I think that meant "welcome"—I was never for sure, because most of my years there, I cleaned the dormitories on the other side of campus. But we saw Black kids—the College didn't have but so many of them—going in and out of that house, so most of us came to remember it as the Black House. I guess we was just old school like that. My last year working there, I cleaned offices instead of dorms, so I was cleaning the English department, right near that house, and even though I said *hey* to some of the young brothers and sisters coming from that house, and even though they was raised right enough to call me by my last name and say *hey* back, I kept calling it the Black House. I suppose I liked that better, 'cause I liked to know that in the middle of that place, there was a house that was for the Black folks.

But it was gone. I got to Hartford Avenue, just across the way, and there was just a hole in the ground. It was square. They filled it in, but I could still see the basement walls, red mud and gray dirt almost to the top. The College had already bought up and took out many buildings. And maybe you had some houses that got burnt out and never built back up. Some landlords didn't want to fool no more with it; got they ass away from us and out to the suburbs, where they say it's safe. But from the other side of the street, I didn't see no mess like somebody wrecked or burnt out that house. It was just gone, like somebody picked it up and they carried it away in they pocket.

I was thinking I was just having troubles, like the doctor said anybody might have when their son gets killed by another boy's bullet. Every thought was coming down on me. I was thinking I worked at the College for ten years, been around there many years before and after that, and that house was always there. Maybe I was thinking it was wrong to see nobody around, too. No students, no workers, no police—like everything was changed up. I walked to the lawn in front of that hole.

When I got closer I saw it wasn't much of a hole. It was almost all filled in, and near the front it was filled right to the top. I looked around, because maybe somebody was messing with me, and I didn't want go be nobody's fool. But it was cold, and nobody was out. I walked to the middle of the empty lot. Nothing but dirt filling a box. I was standing on dirt, but I felt like I was floating; maybe this is where the living room was or the kitchen. I looked up, trying to figure where the bedrooms used to be. When I looked along the foundation I saw edges of wallpaper still on the basement walls—that old-style wallpaper, like in my grandmomma's house—and that alone near set me off, because she had been gone for longer than I wanted to think about. It was red wallpaper, with green-and-blue stripes. I was thinking that somebody needed to finish up, since the job looked like somebody didn't give a damn. They should have filled it in all the way or left all of it showing. Either way, if you make like you doing work, don't do no half-ass job.

There was dirt and basement walls and torn wallpaper, and after that there was the yard around where that house used to be. Past that I saw the dormitories they built last summer, walkways and young bushes and trees, no more than a year old. I didn't come this way much, so I noticed that for the first time. I almost laughed because it was funny to me that they was making like things was on the move when I never would know about it around my way.

I never been to college, and I was never real tight with none of those students, but Donnell was not much older than them. If he was a student up in there and that house was gone like it was, I know he'd be worked up about it. Sometimes you get to feeling things for other people, like their problems could be yours. If you love your children, you could feel for anybody's children, even if they ain't yours. I'm sure people I don't even know feel for Donnell, like the way the sister at the hospital had her hand on Donnell's cheek for a few minutes after he was gone. I couldn't feel a thing at first. That will come. But right then, I was looking at her and felt what she was feeling: She was a mother who was a doctor, and maybe she was thinking *something beautiful is gone out of somebody's life*. I don't know what she was thinking, but when I miss Donnell, I feel some strength when I think on how somebody else was sad to see him go. So me in front of that hole, I was feeling something for somebody right then.

I was going to put my bag down just when I started to see rain, and I knew I had to get on home. That's when I started to feel some sort of sign. I took a piece of that wallpaper, put it in my bag, and stepped back to the curb. I was crossing the street, my head was down, against the rain, and I saw the tire marks, big truck tire tracks all over, from the yard, over the sidewalk, across the grass, curving out and back, many times over into the street, and then on down Hartford Street, almost to where the main College property was closed off from the neighborhood.

There was nobody out, no people, no cars. I walked down the street, following the tire tracks. After a ways down, it was only one set of tracks, and farther down they got back into all those curves and turns, running all over the street again and up onto a lawn and sidewalk, and there it was: the Black House, like nobody touched it, only set it someplace else.

It sat on a new cement foundation. They had unfinished wooden stairs running up to the front door. I had never seen such a thing. By then the rain was on me, and I was already wet. But I was putting it all together: the house, the rain, that wallpaper, me in front of that house, and I there I was, worn from first shift and my boy gone for good. But I also was feeling for those students. It wasn't the same as somebody's boy being shot by accident at the corner store, but that place meant something to those kids. That house used to sit in a visible place. Maybe nobody cared if it meant something or not. Maybe it was no big thing for anybody. But I put in years over there at the College, and something didn't feel right. People just up and move a whole house. Whatever didn't feel right was working on me, and I knew when I got home, that night or next morning, or over the weekend—*come Sunday*, like my momma sings—I'd know what was right.

The B6 had done its route maybe twice by now, and I should have been home. I turned down Hartford Street. I walked through the gate and I knew right then that come Sunday, I was going to be ready to have words with somebody.

———

He looks like a man who has decisions to make, and he doesn't hold himself like a man who wants to hear from me. But he sure enough has out that hand and puts on that smile. It hasn't been a quick breath after his secretary greeted me with the same put-on smile. She had the outside lobby door open for me like I brought somebody greens and pie on Labor Day. Had me by the arm, or it was more like her hand was *near* my elbow but not *on* it; if I didn't go where she had in mind for me to go, I'd know about it, but she wasn't set on touching me, either. We stood there, and I don't think that woman knew what to do next. *You don't need anything, do you?* she said, *I could make something,* but she was already sitting back at her desk. Woman moved too quick.

She made me nervous, and I was already feeling that nobody I knew ever walked in here like the head man of the College better make time to meet with somebody like me. I turned from her to the room. I noticed the mahogany chairs and a coffee table with magazines and newspapers on it. It looks like a living room, like you see set up in storefronts. Nice chairs and rugs, paintings of men who had run the College way back.

I'm trying to remember who cleans this building when here comes the president with that hard smile and his blue blazer and that hand. He leads me into his office just like his assistant led me into the lobby. After the handshake, he's good at not touching me, too. He closes the door and he's still working that smile when he sits down. I stand there to be polite, show some manners, and when he doesn't say anything, I take a seat. I get settled in before he talks because I'm there to say some things. He is holding onto his smile, and I'm hearing Janeece or Miss Petry, from down the block, busting on me cause *who ever got it in her mind to send a ninety-cent Hallmark card telling this man "hey, you and me, we got to talk. I worked this place before you come on, and we need to talk about how I can help you out and you can help me out,"* and maybe that ain't even the crazy part Janeece was worked up about. *Crazy* was calling the man's office every two weeks for three months before the secretary finally said the president could meet with me. When I asked why it took so long, she told me, *The President has a strong commitment to his College-related associations and that makes him a busy man.* I told her I wouldn't be wasting his time. Janeece and Miss Petry wouldn't let me alone—*going up to the College, like you somebody*—and when the both of them said the same thing, I told them both that I could do fine without them.

Now I'm sitting in this office and I starting to feel like *who am I to be up in here?* but I know I got to do right for Donnell.

"So, you're here to help me." He's still smiling.

"I can." I take off my hat.

"And I can help you?"

"Donnell, my boy, he's dead. Gone three and a half months now; another boy was worked up at somebody else and my boy got caught in it."

He puts a hand to his mouth. "Yes, I think I remember hearing about that."

"It didn't make no big news. I had to just get him buried real quick. Didn't have enough for a wake or nothing. It was just him and me."

"There's a lot of that, it seems, and not enough people really care."

"You so right."

"Well, when the College has finished building the Boy and Girls Club, kids will have someplace to go that's safe."

"I'm sure we could talk on that one a while, but you got something you can do now, too. That's why I'm here."

"What's that?"

"Y'all moved that house like *that*, and ain't nobody said a word?"

He looks confused.

"The Black House."

"We call it the *Akwaaba* House. It's *African* for—"

"—Is African a language?"

"Well, actually—"

"All them years and you just up and move it?"

"That move has been a part of our long-term Master Plan for College Development and Community Stabilizing. We want it to be closer to the community."

"Seems like you're moving it farther away from the center of the College. Ain't nobody had nothing to say about it."

That smile is gone for good, and some pink starts rising up in his neck. "The College thought seriously over the move of the House."

"So you didn't have no trouble out of anybody about it?"

"I thought we were talking about your son." He has a pleasant face, but he looks over my shoulder, to above the door. There's a clock there; I used to clean this office, too.

I heard and read about the man over the years. I read in the papers how he had been on city councils and helped folks during the Civil Rights Movement. He liked to tell people that he was a driver for Andy Young. He was good with urban communities, the news said, but since we always heard about his plans and never met the man, I always wondered what that was supposed to mean.

"We are talking about Donnell. And we're talking about that house, too. And we're talking about your Master—what'd you call it?"

"It's the Master Plan for—its a plan to get the College and the community together," he said.

"That's this *long-term Master Plan for College Development and Community Stabilizing,* right? Getting the College and the hood together? I've been thinking on some ways to get folks together. Maybe Black folks up here might want some kind of way to talk about that house, and maybe folks from my way might want to talk about my son, and maybe other people might want to listen."

"I'm not sure I see how the Akwaaba House and your son are related."

"It's just about getting people together, like you say."

"I have put my life into getting people together, and that's what the College is trying to do, but I don't see how I can help your particular case here."

"I know the plans up in here. I got people been working here before you was out of college. Some military college, right? I read the paper. I know."

"Then you should know that I'm about working in the community," and he holds on that *u* when he says *community* and spreads his arms to me, like he'd be down next week to eat wings and play bid whist with Janeece, Miss Petry, and me on my porch.

I wait for him to finish. He goes on about his plan, talking on and on with his hands, and I almost forget that I should be the one doing the talking. But he seems like the sort you have to let talk before he might listen.

"So you should know I'm about good things," he says. "I was a driver for SCLC back in the Movement, and I fought for Asian-American rights when I was in Califor—"

"—What's that got to do with right here?"

"Well, I thought you should know where I'm coming from."

"Sir, I come from Cairo, Georgia, by way of 322 Broad Avenue, right outside your gates."

He looks at me, changing up that face again. It gets soft, and he puts his palms to his desk. "Why don't we get back to your son."

It's right at this moment that I know he's already shut me down. You work long enough for White people—serving them, cleaning up after them—you get to knowing when they stop seeing you and when they not hearing you.

I think about stepping out of there, but it's another hour before I got to be over to work and I don't want to walk back home, so I tell him about Donnell and how he was good to his momma; how he didn't make it to college but he was selling car stereos and learning how to fix them; staying at home, but paying his end on rent. I tell him how Donnell was grown, but a little boy's foolishness was all it took. I talk about how I know there were people who wanted to pay their respects to me and Donnell, but I couldn't have a wake. And then I talk about Janeece's boys, Clay and Ronnie, too young to worry, but too strong-headed to live laughing for long. And I tell the president about Miss Petry and how she been in the neighborhood almost as long as anybody and how she's watched those

College kids smoke their weed up and down the same streets as everyone else. And I talk a bit on the House, because I want to remember that, because maybe those Black students may be dealing with enough up at that College, and somebody's got to say something for them. Their mommas would want that. And I'm not even looking at him, but I figure how many times does somebody like me have a chance to speak their mind to somebody like him, so I tell him how I figured it made sense for the College to let me have a program for Donnell in the Black House, so folks can remember all those things that's changed for good. Just people getting together, to complain or cry, cut up, just to talk. And I finish by saying, *the way I came up, that's how we got folks together*.

He is quiet for a bit, showing me he can be polite. He tells me that "the College has worked through the moving of the House" and he says that it's never just up to him to decide what happens in there. He calls it a *facility*. He says he will check into what can be done, and he'll get back to me, but I'm thinking about how it took me those two months to meet with the man. He gets up, says he's sorry about Donnell. He puts out his hand, we shake, and that's it.

I've got a half hour left before work. I head across the campus, toward the Grounds Department. I know Sammy Webb, who works landscape crew over there. Sammy came up with Donnell, and I fixed him more meals than I knew I had money for; boy ate fried chicken like it was his job. He didn't mind going to work for the College, and he's been there eight years, working his way up. Soon he'll be foreman. I'll go talk to him and then get to work.

At work I'll tell them I need to take two sick days next

week, to take care of some personal things, I'll say. By then I know Sammy will give me a shift with the crew working the land where the Black House used to be. They been working that land the past few weeks, leveled it all out, got the paths through it, and they about to put in the grass sod. When they get done, it'll be a patch of grass students walk over as they go to class. Landscaping is hard work, but with the work I put in over my fifty years, a day of laying sod won't hurt. I'll use the next day to rest up. Besides, Sammy knows what it's like for me without Donnell, and he will say yes when I ask to work that crew. All I got to say is I'm needing some extra dollars, more than they pay you for a day's work at the phone company. He'll get me on that crew and worry how to get me paid in cash by the end of the day.

It's sure to be humid next week, and the sky may look like rain, but it won't. Because I'm not young I'll work the easier job of laying sod, but for just a while—maybe at the end of lunch or afternoon break, I'll borrow a shovel, find a spot near where they just planted a new tree or bush. I'll make me a small hole. Dry dirt makes easy digging. I won't need much space to lay in a few things: a braid from my grandmother's hair, because she was a good soul from way back; a piece of wallpaper from the house; the last paystub I have from the College, the one I cashed in after just one fool too many up there went on about how they gave folks like me a chance to work there. On top of all that I will put a picture of Donnell from when he was in third grade and had a big, gap-tooth laugh so sweet it would break your heart as much as when he slept so still you'd forget he was breathing. I will remember him like that. I will lay some dirt back over that and then a patch of sod, making like that's the area I'm getting to next after the break. It will be me and those men out there, them joking about this old lady putting in work on a humid day. But I've worked the hard jobs, cleaning house, pressing sheets and shirts, raising other people's children, and no matter who it is, when hard work is done, all of us get tired. I'll work with that crew one day, and at knock-off time, when Sammy's reaching in his pocket to pay me, I'll tell him it ain't about the money. I'll tell him I just needed to put in some good work.

For the Brothers
Who Ain't Here

*for William Henry, my namesake
and William Hughes, who carries my name*

I'm on the bus. It's after my shift, and I can't drive the cab where I got to go. The B32 is near full. Hot like the driver forgot what AC was. No seats. I'm the only one standing. People coming from work—all folks from around the way. Feels like everybody keeps looking at me. I keep thinking, *nothing was supposed to happen*. People just staring. I want to say, *hey, ain't nothing supposed to happen*.

Mrs. Wilkes gets on at Eastern Parkway. I see her hat first. Old Sunday hat, off white, fake flowers stuck into the pillbox top. It's tight on her head, but she just about knocks it off working her grocery bags past some kids shoving each other across the aisle. Before I can speak, she starts in.

"Shame what all come down on Ornell."

And I don't have nothing to say, because I already know.

"Super says they got two po-lice outside his door," Mrs. Wilkes says, "but after what Lester done to that child, it ain't like Ornell gonna run out that bed anytime soon. Lord, these children today." And she's done with that. When I don't say nothing back, she makes new creases in her shopping bag. I watch her get off at our block.

I stay on. This ride has been in my head all week, but I held off until now. The route goes by Brooklyn Methodist. That's where they got Ornell.

Nothing was supposed to happen. I could have blamed anybody, and sure, Lester was bound to come looking for who I blamed on messing with his car, but nobody was supposed to get jacked up. I thought of Ornell first because he was easy to blame. Things was always happening to that brother, so folks just figured him for trouble. Somebody's bike get stolen, people put it on him. Your car missing a few days and end up down by the Navy Yards—rims and stereo player gone for good—it must have been Ornell. Even if he was playing dominoes on his stoop or running ball over on Kingston when somebody's place was broken into, they put it on him. Some brothers just get wrote-off like that. But it was no big thing to pin Ornell. Sort of like bullshitting over something that don't work out: The shit never goes down, but the talk is good.

So when word was running the street that I messed with Lester Reece's El Dorado, I dropped the line, *hell, only Ornell Sykes fool enough to be on parole and mess with Lester's El D.* I kicked it like I was shit talking. I didn't stress it. Just said it a couple of times, waiting for the bus and over a game of dominoes in front of Lester's uncle's stoop. One of those times, I know I heard somebody say, *damn right,* and I was thinking the heat was off me.

Lester wasn't the sort of brother to have looking for you. When we were kids, twelve or thirteen years old, Lester was the only one on our block who left his bike unlocked when he was in the corner store. If you were fool enough to take his bike, he would run after you, catch you in two blocks. You didn't want him to catch you. If you peddled fast enough to get away, he'd find you.

He was back on the block after doing ten years in the Army. Lester was linebacker size but he knew he wasn't going to play ball for nobody after high school. So he joined up, studied electronics, kept those choppers going in the first Gulf war. Black brothers fighting Brown brothers for White folks' money wasn't my style, but I had to give it up to Lester. Brother didn't spend a dime when he was joined up. Whatever he wore, ate, drank, smoked, or traded came from the Army. Lester saved his pay and never gambled past half of what he had in his pocket. He set himself straight—living in a two-bedroom place—and when he wasn't in work clothes or shorts, he wore nothing but shirt-and-pant combos. The hat always matched the shoes.

But the Cadillac, that was another thing. Lester put the down payment on the Caddy with his muster-out money, covered the car note with his Con Ed paycheck. That was a serious ride: 1978 El Dorado. Leather seats and two-tone gray— the dark charcoal faded to silver smoke near the wheels. He came back into Brooklyn in that ride, brass Airborne frame around the Vet license plate. Like his cream-and-tan Cutlass he had before he joined up, that Caddy never knew what dirt was. He would jack you up for eyeballing him the wrong way, but messing with that Caddy, that was another thing.

The Knicks was on when his car alarm went off. Lester's Caddy didn't have that small-money, don't-nobody-give-a-fuck alarm you got used to hearing. Lester's shit was loud, like a *siren,* a somebody's-shit-is-burning-down kind of thing. Lester put money into that ride. It was parked in front of my building, right outside my stoop. Sometimes late in the day, he would leave it there, with the windows open, stereo loud so you could hear it a block away. He would make like he was just running inside to take a piss, check on the game. But it was about that car, making sure folks saw him getting in and out of that car. Lester would be inside his place, eating Crown Fried Chicken, playing cards, watching the game. The siren was loud, and I was thinking to myself, *you got to be a damn fool to mess with Lester's ride.* But then the siren faded as the car left our block, and I stopped worrying about it.

Two days later, they found the El Dorado in Bushwick, scratched up on the driver's side and the hubcaps gone, but that was it. Didn't look like theft, more like somebody trying to fuck with Lester. I knew right away folks would put it on me, like I got it in for him. But everybody know I had my fill of Lester years back: I step on his shoes after a ball game, and two broke ribs was enough for me. Me, I never got into no-body's mess no more. I did my hours working my taxi and got my ass home. I don't want no trouble.

Nothing was supposed to happen to Ornell. Lester figured him for a sucker, but they was close. Came up on the same block, years before I moved in. They had that Cooley High–Cornbread Earl sort of thing going. Ornell was like the foolhead kid brother. When Ornell used to come around the way, Lester would shout out, *my li'l brutha!* as soon as he turned the corner. Ornell would ease our way, and even though they only ran into each other once in a while, they caught up like there was no catching up. Big Les, looking like Lawrence

Taylor in leisure suits, and Ornell, with the soles of his work-boots worn out, and creases sewn into his good pair of jeans.

When I heard that siren, I got to thinking, if I put Ornell's name up and down the block, it's *li'l Brutha* who messed with the Caddy, Lester would be off my ass and easy on Ornell. Whenever Ornell got in the wrong mess, Lester set him straight like it was no big thing.

Lester knew how it was for Ornell. After Lester left for the Army, Ornell was in and out of trouble. He moved twenty blocks away. When Ornell was on the block, folks would ask about Lester, but Ornell had nothing to say. Lester was gone, Ornell was here. And after his mess put him in Sing Sing, Ornell was gone, too. After that, whether he was locked down or not, none of us had nothing to say when anybody asked what was up with Ornell.

The last time the cops got him, only his old super had gone to the trial, and it was Mr. Robinson who let us know how they did Ornell. They was going to send him away, no doubt. But that judge was fed up. A packed courtroom all summer, and Giuliani's crackdowns filling his court. *It was nothin' but brothers up in there*, super said, *all small-shit tickets*. I knew about that. I been there before: I was drinking a beer on my stoop. It was the end of a shift. I made good tips. Cop rolled up, slowed down, checked me like this nigger with a brew on the stoop is stressing the crime rate. He looked at me. I looked at him. He slowed his car. I didn't look away. I was at home, right? On the block where I lived, not where he lived. *What's in the bottle?* he asked. *Something I paid for*, I said. He got out. I stood up. The club was in his left hand. His right was already at the cuffs. They rode me around for six hours in the back of a police van before they locked me down for the night. Nobody said nothing about why I got cuffed. I saw the judge. I paid a fine for the "open-bottle offense." That's all they gave me.

That's the way the mayor gets down in Bed-Stuy. Paper work and long hours to lock down kids on small-time shit. *Ornell fit right in,* Mr. Robinson said about the sentencing, *but five nickel bags of weed don't add up to no longtime sentence. Judge went light on Ornell.* Two years in and one year parole: Sing Sing and a halfway home instead of the big house at Attica.

Everybody knew about the halfway house but his mom. Ornell wanted it that way. He never let her come to court. When he got moved to a halfway house up in Queens, they had him on curfew, a year wearing a LoJack on his ankle. He step too far from where they put him, they lock him back up. But I heard Ornell was back on the block a few times when the days got warm. He'd be around the way, trying to make it happen on the corner. He had cornrows instead of the fade he had when he was locked down, but from a block away you could spot his stride—that loose-hip, Richard Pryor limp step had you laughing when you wanted to beat him down. Jive-ass Ornell.

He never stayed for long. But I wasn't thinking on that. What I planned on was this: Lester knew how it was for Ornell. Lester was back from the Army weeks before his car was stolen, and Ornell got released from Sing Sing a few months before Lester got back on the block. If Lester was thinking Ornell was on parole in Queens, that was all there was to it. They'd find the Caddy; Lester had him some money to fix it up. Lester was in Brooklyn, Ornell was in Queens; that's too much traffic just to beat somebody's ass. Besides, if Lester started in on him, things could be hard for Ornell. They start something up, the police would come. Cops always come.

And they already got their pound out of Ornell when they locked him down for those two years after they caught him pushing herb outside the Nostrand Avenue station. People watched them work him over the hood of a car, and his head was all bust open, seemed like nobody give a damn. Folks across Fulton Street was laughing, and when it got rough, they got quiet. Turned away. Wrote it off as everyday shit. Everybody around the way knew Ornell wasn't about nothing. But them special unit cops, they got something to prove, and Ornell was fool enough to be selling herb right where they was on us. The Man, up in our spot, at every subway stop—Fort Greene-Lafayette, Franklin Avenue, Nostrand, Utica Avenue. Every few blocks on the weekends. Giuliani don't say it, but he don't give a fuck about the brothers, so his boys don't neither. They don't mind if we get put under, but they steady on us when we walking free. Ornell should know better—head up Nostrand a ways, under the elevated tracks, and sling that shit as people walk by. But Ornell was *runnin bizniss*, like he used to say. He was working the rush hour, folks coming and going from the train stop, and he's hustling, talking to no one and to everyone passing by: *smoke, smoke, brother need a smoke?* Talking low, but too damn bold to be so shady.

Plainclothes cops rolled him hard out on that street. It was just *herb*. And everybody know Ornell don't carry much, and what he do carry crumble like dry shit on a hot day. So everybody on the block was laughing, because who figures a brother get locked down for five nickel bags of weed, and who figures they hold Ornell's old record against him: You aint a "threat to society" because some appliances fall off a truck in Garden City and you resell them in Brownsville without a receipt. Even if you done it more than once. That's some stupid shit, but it ain't Alcatraz time.

Nobody was thinking he was in for nothing but a fine and that don't-you-act-like-the-nigger-I-know-you-are look from the judge. Even Ornell was smiling, figured it was a week's pay he'd write off to the mayor. That's how everybody saw it going down. But they sent him away.

He done his time. Started working the Queens gig. Walking tall with that LoJack on his leg. It's one thing to be like them Brothers on chain gangs down South, that's some hard-rock shit. But that LoJack kept Ornell from running just the same.

We all knew he was around the way every so often, but most times I forgot he was around. We try not to lose track. When it came time to open the beer on the stoop, somebody always poured some on the sidewalk, *for the brothers who ain't here.* And that's when we remember: For Lester, when he was away in the Army. For Whitney Phillips, shot and gone five years now. For Danny Witts, locked up at fifty-five for putting the hurt on a White man trying to rob his store. Tariq Hayes, who left for college and never came back. Victor Figueroa, only *boriqua* to live in the Black folks' hood where he ran his store, shot over two six packs. The Washington boys, locked down for life. Cliff Brooks, up at Attica for ten. Denard Williams. Dre Bennett. Ornell Sykes.

They let him out, but they kept him in Queens, away from home. We could all understand him stealing away to Brooklyn now and then, just trying to make it back to where you from.

Nobody cared much for him, but nobody said nothing if they saw him breaking parole. Nobody wants to see a brother go to the big house.

Most times I heard about him after he was gone. You'd hear he was around the way after he had come through. He never told his mom when he was around; he stayed away from her building. He was going to surpise her when he got his shit together. I didn't give him much thought until I heard that car siren, and then all I had in my mind was Lester, looking for *me*.

I heard the next day if it wasn't me who messed with the car, I must know who did. I figured Lester will come looking for me, thinking, *how that nigger gonna mess with my ride when he know I beat his ass before?* Lester didn't check for facts. He'd be coming for me. My name being in the mix was enough. So my answer was easy. And I figured Lester would go light on Ornell. It was small shit. He wouldn't be so hot about his car; probably have the dents out and chrome spoke wheels back in place before a week could pass.

Lester's car was back on the block by Monday last week. New green gloss finish. Gold spoke wheels. Word was Lester was cruising that car slow, looking for Ornell. And I'm thinking, Ornell in Queens; Big Les is just flexing. He was riding the long blocks between Classon and Nostrand, along Fulton and past the Kingston courts. At first I didn't worry on it much; Ornell supposed to be in Queens. Shouldn't be messing with that curfew. Even if he was fool enough to be caught around the way, Ornell was tight with Lester. *Li'l Brutha*. Ain't no big thing.

But now Ornell is laid out at Methodist, all fucked up, with the police outside his door. The super went to visit him first. Mr. Robinson waited an hour before they let him see Ornell. Said Ornell be in there at least a week more. *Boy breathin' like a tore-out muffler.* Eye swollen shut. Jaw broke. Can't piss. *A body heal up, though,* Mr. Robinson was saying, *he got longer pains after that.*

I wanted to go on the first day he could have visitors. What was I going to tell the brother? He should have been in Queens: The Man put you away from your home, it must be for a reason. Stay in line, or stay in trouble.

You was supposed to be in Queens, brother. That's what I figure I got to say to Ornell when I see him. But by the time I get through hospital security, to the elevators and I'm on my way up, I know it ain't about Queens.

The El Dorado. Every brother deserves to have a car like that. Seat tilted back, cruising the Ave in the Caddy, the Intruders on the radio. Wash that thing three times a week. Rolling from Bed-Stuy to Bushwick, looking for cookouts to drive past. Every day feels like a Saturday when you drive like that.

My every day was other people's fares. Midtown to LaGuardia. LaGuardia to Hunt's Point. Over to Washington Heights. To 115th and St. Nicholas. Hundred and fourth and Amsterdam. Central Park West and 79th. Lexington and 34th. Park Avenue to East Village. Alphabet City. LaGuardia.

I got to thinking, *I done my time.* I kept out of jail. Didn't fool with the brothers on the corner. I did my thing in school. Finished on time. I thought about college, but all I needed was that one day in the drugstore, when I had my Sunday suit on for the interview at City College and they still watched me like I was going to steal something. College wouldn't smooth that out, no matter how nice my suit was. And I wasn't going to say, *you want fries with that?* for the rest of my life.

The cab suited me fine at first. I figured I was going wherever it was I wanted. I decided who rode or who didn't. Maybe I drive fast for you, because you understand that I'm doing something *you need me* to do. Or maybe you think this cab is all I got, so I drive slow. Maybe it takes thirty minutes to make a twenty-minute ride. Maybe you're late to that meeting, miss a train. You already wrote me off, so why should I step 'n' fetch for you? That was my style.

Eight years of busting it in that cab, and I catch myself one day thinking, *I'm driving a cab; this is what I do.* I was stuck in traffic on the Manhattan Bridge—White man and his wife needed to be at JFK in twenty minutes. I picked him and wifey up in midtown, Lexington and 35th: *here's another twenty, just get us there!* and you goddam right we made it. *Thank you, my man,* he said when the bags were on the curb, *wonderful work.* I had to smile at that: *my man.* Wifey kicked that Sally Struthers smile like she was proud I had passed my learn-at-home test for taxicab drivers. And I drove off, fingering a twenty-dollar tip, thinking I had the rest of the day to do the same damn thing. *This is what I do.* I said that all day.

When I got home, I had the Miller Hi-Life in the fridge, Clyde Frazier was calling the game on the radio, and the Knicks were up: Ewing fouled out, Starks was working a double-double. At the half, I stepped into the front hall to finish my beer on the stoop. Lester had just rolled up from getting ribs. I saw him from behind the glass of my building front door. I walked out as he went in the next building. He didn't see me, so I didn't say hello. When I got outside, a breeze was rolling down the street. I sat on the stoop, and the smell of the ribs was drifting from the car. Lester left the stereo on and the windows down. He was inside his apartment, eating ribs, waiting for the game to come back on. The Delfonics were on the radio. DJ was singing over the music, between songs, *ready or not, here I come, you can't hide, I'm gonna find you and make you love me* . . . "Old School," they call it now. The Caddy was just sitting there. Lester had just waxed it that day. He had this gold L swinging from the key he left in the ignition. I finished two beers looking at that Caddy.

Six long blocks away, Lester's car alarm finally cut off. I drove down Fulton, over to Myrtle, past the courts at Fort Greene Park. On Flatbush, I tilted the wheel down and eased the seat back as I rolled with the Jeeps and Range Rovers driving from the Manhattan Bridge out to Bay Ridge. I drove around Prospect Park and down Eastern Parkway, got a sandwich on Bedford and ate it in the park across from the Navy Yards. By the time I drank my fourth beer, I felt like I'd never drive another damn cab for nobody.

I got to tell Ornell I didn't see all of what happened to him, but I was there when it went down. I was off my shift, buying beer down in the corner store. I wasn't going out much that week. Folks said Lester was looking for Ornell, but I wasn't taking chances. Lester was no joke after the Army: leaner from basic, but stronger from lifting when he wasn't working the choppers. I got my hundred and eighty pounds, but Lester's lean two twenty is still don't-fuck-with-me size. I was coming out of the store when Lester's car rolled up and then sped past. The tires made marks. He was already past me, but I stepped back into the store anyway. I heard car horns and I looked down the block. Lester's car was halfway in the parking lane, halfway in the street. Two cars were behind; a bus was on the way. Nobody could pass. The door to the Caddy was open.

I saw people running across the street, and when I looked, there was Ornell, on the pavement. Lester was kicking him. By the time I saw that, it was over. Somebody was shouting, *why you gotta do a brother like that?* Lester turned on them, and they stepped off. The car horns stopped after that. Nobody went near Ornell until Lester backed his car into the street and drove off. Ornell was spread out like he fell down somebody's front stoop. His head was bleeding and his legs spread out on the steps. When I got closer, I saw he was shaking. His radio was broken all up and down the steps. He was trying to get up, see where his boom box was at. He bought it when he was locked down. The first day I see him back—not more than three months into parole—he was playing dominoes with the super in front of the laundromat on Bedford Avenue. Supposed to be on curfew in Queens, but there he was, back in Bed-Stuy, slamming dominoes like he was on vacation. I was thinking, *he's a damn fool,* but, the Bones was flowing for him and his box was under the table, busting the Isley Brothers down Bedford Avenue. He was singing—*It's your thang*—scoring twenty-five points—*now what you wanna do?* He kept singing the same song—*I can't tell ya*—on last domino, he slapped down a double blank—*who to sock it to . . .* Before he even got out of Rikers, everybody knew he folded eight thousand sheets to save for that radio. I could hear the ambulance siren coming from Eastern Parkway, but nobody was helping Ornell. He was looking for the box. He kept saying *Where's my jams?* A speaker was in his hand. He kept trying to pick up the rest.

I see the cops as soon as I step from the hospital elevator. They were looking for me before I got off. I got maybe a forty-yard walk before I step up to them, to see if they let me talk to Ornell. I'm walking, and it's like being back on the block on a summer night. I'm walking home from the corner store or from ball at Kingston. I got forty yards to go—the end of one block and the intersection—before I'm on my block. But there they go: blue uniform all square and tight over the bulleproof vest. It's where we live, but they on top of us, like we already done something wrong. They look at me nervous; I get nervous. What would they do? The two guarding Ornell's room, they don't want to hear about why Ornell's all fucked up. *Shouldn't be running off.* That's all they got to say.

I'm going to tell them I only need to talk to Ornell for five minutes. I got to step into that room and tell him, *say brother, it was me who done you like this.* And I got to stay there when he gets heated about that. I got to look right at him if all he does is cry. Not every day somebody will listen to that. I'm halfway to his room and I want to say, *nothing was supposed to happen,* but I know that's just part of it.

And now I think I will go in, sit there, make myself look at Ornell. If I had the money, I'd bring him a new radio, and he'd still be bullshitting, like, *I already got one, my man. Needs some fixin'. I give it up cheap, ten dollars, az-iz.* It would be nice like that, start up fooling around, but I know it won't swing that way. I got to sit there. And if he says *why you gotta do me like this?* I have to sit there and try to say something, before the cops say it's time to go.

But they not going to let me in. They watch me from down the hall. They already got me figured out before I walk up. Why they going to let me in? Mayor Giuliani says they got to be polite, say, *yes sir* and *no ma'am,* but they know who's running things. I want to say *this is a hospital,* but that ain't nothing. For them, we just back on the block: I walk up. They call in, check me out. They pat my clothes for something hard or sharp. They will act like they seen me before. They seen all of us before. They will take their time. They will break down the questions. *Who are you? Where you going? Where you coming from? Why are you here? Why don't you move along?*

Why We Jump

for Dieudonne

When Lynette Simmons sees Samuel Cates for the first time in twenty-five years she is not sure if it is the Mr. Cates she remembers. She's on the train home, Green Line to Columbia Heights, when she sees him. He stands facing the darkness of the metro tunnel, rushing past the double door windows. He fidgets, clutches his bag, shifts his weight, anxious for the next station. When he lifts his head to look at the reflection of the people in the car, she sees his face. Lynette recognizes the small ears and the thin, carefully kept mustache. Mr. Cates, the man who, when she was twelve, took a running leap from the floor above her apartment and crashed through the deck roof her daddy had just built. The apartments were terraced: The Simmons's family-size apartment on the fourth floor pushed beyond the outer wall of the fifth floor, where a two-foot ledge jutted out from the large windows of Mr. Cates's single-unit apartment. Talk got around the building that he was trying to make it to the alley, five floors down. That meant a talented leap past the Simmons's small deck, and though he took to it as if it were his only way out, he never made it. Sammy Cates, whom she hasn't seen since.

He gets off at L'Enfant Plaza station. Before reasoning on the wisdom of it, she follows him as he heads for the Blue Line. Mr. Cates carries a faded Washington Bullets bag under his arm as he rides the escalator from the platform. His wool blazer looks tailored, recently pressed, with whale-bone buttons. The back of his shirt collar—for that's all she can see after he has turned from her—is clean but frayed. *Too much bleach*, she thinks to herself. As he rises, she holds back, takes notice of his shirt collar, blazer, then his pressed, well-worn khakis and running shoes.

She eases onto a bench, rests her grocery bags, catches her breath before she decides to proceed. For a moment she's disturbed: She feels unsettled in having seen him but doesn't know why. She wants to feel that seeing Mr. Cates is a sign— a *revelation*, as folks at church might call it; an *incarnation,* as she'd like to call it—but of what? There are gaps and voids in how she has imagined him. She can't abide by what has slipped her mind for so long, and in this forgetfulness sits herself down longer than she would like. Lynette Simmons gets this way when the what-should-be of her life clashes with the what-is. Like when she finds herself frozen at the breakfast table, spoon in hand, cereal in the bowl, no milk in the fridge. But she has three cartons of juice, five boxes of cake mix, enough canned beans for ten meals—supplies that a fixed shopping list provides. Everything but milk, which, because she always buys it, she leaves off the list, along with tampons and coffee.

———

She remembers that day, twenty-five years ago, as a hot one. Most of the days she recalls from childhood were hot, when sweat came from double dutch and bicycle races, when she heard the off-key warble of the ice cream truck more often than the wail of sirens. If she ever explains that day to anyone, she knows she would start with the heat; the day was hotter than most she remembers. It was the heat that made folks crazy: Kids dropping bricks onto Military Road from the Sixteenth Street overpass, rich White folks cursing at each other on the sidewalk in Georgetown. The police were everywhere, it seemed, busy with arresting someone or wanting to. It was hot all over D.C., even up on Meridian Hill, where a breeze might catch you by surprise.

The Orioles game had just gone off the air. Her father was turning ribs on the grill. Her mother had been out for cigarettes and beer to replace what Lynette's father and her Uncle Norman had already drunk. Lynette was mixing instant ice tea in the kitchen. Auntie Berthine, from across the hall—more close friend than blood aunt—was over to visit, along with her cousin, Odessa, from down the street. When Berthine wasn't teasing Lynette's father about his sorry Orioles, she was on Lynette about how much she didn't carry herself like the girl she was supposed to be. When her mother wasn't around, Berthine and Odessa took turns working their finishing-school ideals into Lynette. They called it baby-sitting. On that day they were sitting on the deck like two doves—pretty dark eyes and big breasts on the both of them. They worked the dozens on Lynette's father while he looked after the ribs and Uncle Norman finished off the beer.

Lynette was bringing the pitcher of iced tea out to the deck when she heard heavy footsteps running above their living room ceiling, two heavy steps toward the outside wall and then down came Mr. Samuel Cates, through the green deck roof and right onto her father's lounger.

All of them looked to the hole in the roof first. Through that hole, Lynette could see the top of the window of Mr. Cates's apartment. He didn't have a deck like the Simmons's apartment, just a small ledge and a railing.

Then they looked to Mr. Cates. The pitcher tipped in Lynette's hands as she looked him over; and she spilled ice tea down her front before dropping the pitcher. It broke, but no one seemed to care about that.

Blood trickled from the top of Mr. Cates's head to his temple. He kept his hair cut close to the skin, and that made the gash in his head look larger than it really was. Lynette had already made a hobby of observing Samuel Cates. In her little girl's mind, it was spying; that was more exciting. She might catch a glimpse of him in the laundry room of the building or, standing on the elevator with her mother in between them, she would crane her head ever so slightly to stare at his hands. His fingernails were pristinely kept. Her daddy's carried thin lines of dirt nearly every day other than Sunday.

She mostly saw Mr. Cates from behind, awkwardly backing on to the elevator to avoid eye contact, or rushing out of the building and down the street; he was always in a hurry. But now he was right in front of Lynette. Her mother wasn't there to scold her for staring. It seemed to her that she never had a chance to look at anyone for long. But now he was in the middle of her deck, dazed and bleeding. He was wearing a tan suit-coat and pants, a nice tie to match, though the collar of his shirt was red with blood. But right then, none of that seemed strange to her.

By the time Lynette rises from the bench, Mr. Cates is stepping from the escalator to the Blue Line platform. She catches a glimpse of his black socks and running shoes. Those surprise her, the running shoes. More than surprised, she's curious. She heads for the Blue Line.

For years she had imagined him in worsted-wool slacks and loafers. She deduces that the running shoes support all the walking he must do from place to place. He doesn't own a car; it's been years since he stopped driving. She decided this a long while back. She imagined he didn't drive because he is a man who distracts easily, making esoteric the mundane of what's around him: faulty green light, flickering rather than solid; road construction sign, bent so that it reads SLOW MEN; flurry of pigeons across the reflection of a sedan's tinted windows; the wide eyes of four children in a bus, staring at the pigeons; a fifth child, two seats back, fascinated with a feather the flurry has cast to the wind. No, driving would be too risky for Samuel Cates. He'd be watching that feather or absorbed with the child, watching the feather, and sideswipe somebody's car. Then he'd have to deal with that. She's certain he's cut out the risk of accidents he can't afford or attention he'd rather not face.

Mr. Cates lay there on the deck, blood staining his shirt collar. But as red as that collar got, no one moved. Lynette remembers how still everyone became. Except for her father, who was cursing into the alley. Mr. Cates's surprise landing had bounced the ribs from the grill into a Dumpster below. Mr. Simmons looked back to Lynette and then glared at Mr. Cates, who wasn't focused on much of anything. Her father threw the grill fork into the alley, and they heard it clatter in the Dumpster.

That's when it looked like Mr. Cates suddenly knew where he was. He rubbed his head. Blood smeared over half his face. For a moment his eyes got big and then rolled back. He shook himself, got his face straight, and said, "I'm sorry."

Berthine began laughing so hard that she fell back in her chair. Then Norman and Odessa busted out laughing. Lynette knew that if her mother was there, no one would be laughing. Avis Simmons was a graceful, serious woman, the kind who, Lynette felt, never did the wrong thing.

She knew laughing was the wrong thing. She was a quiet girl, a child who would get called out by her teacher for getting lost in pictures in her math book more so than the math or the dove-shaped birthmark on the neck of the girl who sat next to her. She would hear the teacher's voice from far off— *Lynette Simmons, close your mouth before a fly moves in!* At recess and lunch, kids would stare at her and mock her openmouthed fascination with things they had missed. She wished she could say something to stop Berthine and the rest from laughing, but Berthine had a sharp tongue that Lynette did not want to challenge.

Lynette's father went to help Mr. Cates. "Sammy Cates! What's in your mind, bustin' up my damn roof like that?"

Mr. Cates didn't answer.

"I just put the damn thing on this past April!" her father was saying, "And look at my chair! How am I gonna fix that?"

Uncle Norman was saying, "How we gonna eat?"

Mr. Cates loosened his tie. He was looking at Lynette, and she was reminded of the stares she received from the men at the bus stop on Georgia Avenue, the way they looked her up and down with tight-lipped smiles, feeling something she did not. They weren't like the boys her age, who were too busy rubber-necking at titties to notice anything special about her. Though his lips were tight, Mr. Cates's stare was different.

Berthine, who was watching this exchange, hooted to Lynette, "Honey, Sammy Cates ain't looking at nothing you ain't even growed yet!" Lynette laughed a little, feeling some tingle there, on the skin of her chest, or maybe just inside, because more than embarrassment or fear, she felt warm with fascination.

She wondered if he knew who she was. There were times when she felt that only her mother and Berthine noticed her, and that was usually to criticize. Surely Mr. Cates had noticed her in the laundry room, on the elevator, or playing in the courtyard of the building.

Now, on her deck, Mr. Cates smiled at Lynette—gently, a pastor's smile—as if he could just smile away her troubles. She thinks now how odd that was: him sitting there, bruised and bleeding, looking certain that everything would work out. She smiled back, but then his face got serious, like he was apologizing again.

———

The Blue Line heads to Springfield. Samuel Cates stands facing the subway door. Lynette sits where she can study his profile. He stoops more than stands. He reminds her of Everton Fox, the weatherman she sometimes catches when she watches the BBC. She's embarrassed that Everton Fox comes to mind—her, a girl from Meridian Hill, Chocolate City born and bred, watching the BBC like some Embassy Row highbrow. If she had a group of Friday-night-at-the-hair-salon-girlfriends to trade stories with, she'd tell them, *Everton looks like a filled-out Billy Dee. I know he must love him some ribs and greens* . . . and she'd lean into a friend's hip while they both doubled over, so her TV crush would seem more like girl talk than fantasy. She smiles for a moment, because she'd like some Fridays to be like that.

But why would Everton Fox come to mind? He's nothing like Mr. Cates—Cates is small-boned and stooped; he has salt-and-pepper hair, with a less satisfied stomach than Fox—and what is she embarrassed about? She can't say for sure.

She puts her grocery bag between her feet. She has just the one now; the meats, ice cream, and milk she left on the bench. She is not sure where Mr. Cates is headed, but it's sure to be far enough for cold foods to spoil. She's particular about such things, how long eggs are out of the fridge, whether potato salad sits in sun or shade. These concerns she's carried from her mother's house, a place where bed sheets were ironed and hair was always pressed, elbows and knees glistened with Vaseline, and children answered with *yes, ma'am* rather than *yeah*. She lives in the same building she grew up in. Sixth floor now instead of fourth. Two bedrooms, with a southern view of downtown. Low-rent high-rise, a few blocks from Malcolm X Park. The City's salary allows her that much. Six floors in Meridian Hill, tallest hill in the city, is higher than ten stories near Georgetown. Prime real estate if White folks lived near Brown folks.

Where does Samuel Cates live now? It's just past rush hour on a Friday, so she figures he must be headed home, somewhere along where the Blue Line snakes through North West D.C. or Virginia. Or is it north of Georgetown? Does he got it like that? This is a movin'-on-up step she can't reconcile. She has never known what he did for a living, but she also hasn't figured him as a suburban type. She's known folks who moved into Landover, Rockville, Prince George's County, where the cul-de-sacs, condo rows, and ranch styles look like the suburbs, but the people lived it like the best and worst of South East D.C. Folks moved out to P.G. County, Bowie, Wheaton when they got their money together or wanted to look like they had money to get together. When Lynette was young, she did not think of Mr. Cates as a man with money. He almost always wore white button-down shirts, no tie, no suit. Sometimes his shirts were wrinkled. On weekends he wore blue button-downs. She saw him in a T-shirt only once. Maybe he managed a store or was an orderly in some clinic. None of that matches up with the Mr. Cates headed into North West: That didn't feel right, even when she considers the worsted wool and loafers she has dressed him in for twenty years. Folks don't just up and move from the hood to Georgetown, do they?

But Mr. Cates was always hard to place. He lived alone. He was a well groomed man, but never wore a suit. No one knew how he paid his rent or could pin down his schedule. When Lynette and her mother would see him, her mother always asked him over for dinner or to visit their church. That was Avis Simmons's way; she didn't like to see people lonely. But each time, Mr. Cates would start in with some excuse, his voice trailing off into a mumble that no one could understand.

Lynette used to steal glances as he sorted through his mail at the elevator doors. He had all sorts of mail: cookware catalogues, coupon books, small boxes from music clubs, brightly colored oversize envelopes. Sometimes Lynette would see a stray envelope or catalogue on a table or windowsill in the lobby and want to pick it up, but her mother wouldn't allow it.

Samuel Cates stares into the dark of the Metro tunnel. Lynette watches his face for signs, a scar, furrowed brow, a furtive look of worry or elation. When she was younger she imagined that, after his jump, such a man would have a twitch or would hold his head to one side, eyes leveled at your shoes or just past your face if conversation was unavoidable.

Now he clutches his Washington Bullets bag. Lynette has not thought of him as a basketball fan. Or perhaps the bag just suits what he has to carry. *What's in the bag?* Books, old newspapers, empty Tupperware he's left too long in the break room fridge at work, shoes—the loafers, perhaps—uniform, gift for his children, frozen dinner, car alternator, a gun? The bulge against the cloth looks like anything and gives away nothing. *Sammy Cates, what's in the bag?*

———

She remembers how after Mr. Cates had been smiling at her for too long, her daddy said, "Go on inside and change your shirt, girl," but she knew he said it just to sound like a father. She didn't move.

Her father then tried to help Mr. Cates to his feet, but Mr. Cates said he was fine. Mr. Simmons said he could *give a got-damn* about how Mr. Cates felt, and went on about his lounger and his deck roof. Odessa helped Berthine get up. Uncle Norman picked the last beer from the cooler, went to look at the ribs in the Dumpster, and whistled like he'd just seen a car accident. He rubbed his chest and lifted his nose to the breeze, which brought with it the smell of chicken frying at Wings-'n'-Things, over on Georgia Avenue.

Lynette had stretched the tea-soaked shirt from her skin and bent down to pick up the broken pitcher. There was still a little ice tea left in the bottom half. She poured it through the wooden planks of the deck, watched the liquid trickle away into the shadows, and waited to hear it hit the drain at the edge of the deck. Lynette heard the front door of the apartment close and her mother drop bags on the coffee table before she stepped past Lynette and onto the deck.

Avis Simmons looked over the scene on the deck and said, "What in the hell is going on?"

Uncle Norman said, "Sho' ain't supper," and tried to keep from laughing.

Maybe they thought Mrs. Simmons was joking, but she wasn't laughing. She was looking at Mr. Cates, who wasn't laughing either.

Mr. Simmons helped Mr. Cates lean against a post and then stepped back.

All the while Uncle Norman was smiling. He eased against the rail and chuckled, "Maybe if you knowed how to stand the fuck up, you might make it to the got-damn alley!"

You see, Mr. Cates was hard to help. It wasn't that he was overweight or weak, but he was uncoordinated. He was dizzy, and he was bleeding, and he was the quiet man from upstairs whom everyone saw but no one knew. And it seemed to Lynette that since Mr. Cates wasn't dead, Norman didn't care if he was hurt or embarrassed.

Mrs. Simmons said, "Hot today, ain't it?" She could have been talking to anyone.

But Mr. Cates said, "Yeah. It is."

Lynette's father looked up through the jagged hole in the roof and said, "Like that's some damn news!"

Berthine and Odessa clasped each others' hands to keep from bursting out again.

"It's Saturday, Samuel," Lynette's mother said. "Why you wearing your Sunday suit?"

Where has he been all this time? Lynette should know about where he's been. Knowing how people are living is her job. She's worked in Children's Welfare at Health and Human Services a long time, long enough to give more instructions than she gets. Last year, they promoted her to an office—same desk in the same corner of the room where she's worked the last twelve years, but now the desk sits behind a metal door and opaque glass partition. Lynette keeps scores of cases in her head. Most are difficult. Many impossible. A dozen or so have set her to crying at the kitchen table before she goes to work.

A few she carries with her long after they have grown up, moved away, died young, or been locked down. She watches how people live. Though she swears herself from forecasting, she feels she has a keen sense for how people's lives will turn out.

There's not a soul Lynette can think of to call on evenings or weekends, but she believes she is a people person. Not the sort who socializes over cocktails and bid-whist. The sort who knows peoples' cousins, godmothers, and deacons. She knows who's in the hospital, who just got out, who's pregnant, divorced, or both. From the time that she moved back into the building, she has followed the passing of elders, families growing, moving in, moving out. She knows well only the people on her floor, but she knows about most who live in the building. Lynette Simmons, who hasn't a gossip mate or phone pal, knows that Elvin and Tracy, the Brevard boys from the second floor, sneak girls into their momma's place during school hours. She knows that the entire fourth floor had been rented by Salvadorans until Immigration cleared them out. She knows the gossip on the Super's new Lincoln: *somebody's wife bought that car*. She has watched the Elkins family move from the back of the first floor to the front of the fifth, and finally to the large corner unit on the third.

Lynette would like to be certain that she saw Mr. Cates sometime after the day he jumped. But she has forgotten. After that day, she would steel her preteen nerves when entering the elevator and quickly press the button for her floor. Sometimes she hoped for a short trip if Mr. Cates was already in the elevator, riding from the basement where he bundled newspapers or placed wrapped trash at the bottom of the Dumpster.

If he wasn't in the elevator, she might hold her arm across the doors for a moment, for sometimes she dared herself to bump into him by chance. But she can't remember when she stopped seeing him in the elevator: Was she twelve? Sixteen? So much of it blurs together.

She has often tried to pin down when he moved out of the building. Sometimes, when she is preparing for bed, she gets it in her mind that it wasn't that she saw Mr. Cates less but that she simply stopped looking out for him. She remembers that it was sometime in her high school years that she began to imagine her own Mr. Cates—Mr. Cates as a librarian or dentist; grown man with no family no friends; his weekends spent in the Smithsonian.

Metro Center station is approaching. Mr. Cates adjusts his grip on the bag before stepping off the train. Lynette follows, quick steps to keep up, a few moments rest on a bench, to ease her eagerness. *It's not the forgetting,* she comforts herself. Everybody forgets. It's the misremembering that causes the void. Because she's not sure what to think next, she tells herself that she has *misremembered* this Mr. Cates, mistaken how he should have looked for someone else, Everton Fox, for example—if he were slimmer—or an old professor, or the produce man at the grocery store who smiles but never speaks.

Mr. Cates heads for the Red Line, bound for Shady Grove. Still traveling west and north. Where's he going? Chevy Chase? Bethesda? *That man don't live in no Chevy Chase,* she thinks. *Folks who live in Chevy Chase don't ride Metro.* Rockville makes more sense. Red Line to Rockville or Twinbrook. Ground-floor apartment, she imagines, two bedroom on a row of cinder-block condos. It's full of old newspapers and clumps of cat hair, which explains why he picks at his blazer like a teen obsessed with zits. She checks her watch to time how long he preens his clothes. Lynette smiles at the intensity of his gestures—traits she would find both annoying and precious in a spouse.

Lynette had sat at the kitchen table while her father and Norman argued in the living room about what to do with Mr. Cates. Berthine and Odessa were on the couch, watching Lynette's father and Norman do little but talk. Her mother was on the deck, with Mr. Cates.

Lynette watched her mother wipe the blood from Mr. Cates's face. He had taken off his suit jacket, and her mother was working at getting him to take off his shirt, to see if he had any other injuries. He didn't want that. When she reached for his buttons, he took hold of Mrs. Simmons's wrist and wouldn't let go. Mr. Cates looked from her face to her hands and then away, looking for somebody might be watching. His neck loosened and he ran his forehead along Momma's hand. She gently eased one of his hands from her wrist and with her other hand she lifted his head up to wipe it.

Norman was trying to get her father worked up. "What if that crazy nigger try something on your wife," Norman said toward the TV.

"Sammy Cates ain't the man to pull that kinda shit." Her

father was talking to the TV, too, " 'sides, if he tried anything, way Avis is, he wish he did hit the alley. Crazy-ass negro, all he is."

In all her life Lynette saw her father push her mother only once. When that happened, Avis Simmons picked herself up, went to the bathroom, closed the door, and didn't come out until long after supper. But early Thursday morning, long before he woke, she took the bolt key from his ring. Her father never noticed and after he left for work in the evening her mother bolted the front door until Sunday. Lynette never knew where her father went, but he came back with cherry blossoms in his hand, singing Donny Hathaway songs from the alley. All Mrs. Simmons ever said was, . . . *on the third day, he rose up and came into his right mind,* and Lynette never saw any more pushing.

Norman and Mr. Simmons sipped at their beer and waited to see what her mother was going to do. Berthine and Odessa were chattering back and forth to each other. Berthine said something about hoping Mr. Cates didn't die or else she wouldn't have a good story to tell after Sunday-morning service, and Odessa said Berthine should be ashamed of herself: God was looking down on all of them. But Berthine was already figuring out, come Sunday, who she would gossip to first.

Mr. Cates gets off at Dupont Circle. This surprises Lynette, so much so that she nearly misses making it off the train. She was settled in for a longer ride. She had been lost in her thoughts, as people often are on long train rides: lost in spy novels, classifieds, and box scores—eyes closed, bopping their heads to the music spinning from disk to headphones—or sitting blank and glassy eyed, casting their worries and daydreams into the darkness beyond the windows. Lynette, thinking Mr. Cates's stop was a long way off, was somewhere in that darkness. It was Mr. Cates's sudden absence from the train doorway that snapped her back to focus, and then she was rushing between the Metro car's closing doors to follow where he must have gone.

She stands on the platform, getting her bearings. Mr. Cates is already rising to the top of the first escalator that will take him out of the station. She gives him some time and follows only after he's stepped off the short escalator leading away from the platform. Lynette watches him slip through the exit gates and toward the escalator to the street. With Samuel Cates several steps ahead, she begins to climb the stairs of the escalator, ascending through the long concrete tube of the Metro exit, its end a bowl of dark, bruise-colored sky into which commuters seem to fall as they step off the top of their ride and go their way. Lynette pauses, looks up at the sky, the dimmed haze of city air waiting to meet her as she rises into it. Mr. Cates steps off, and his head dips out of sight.

When she reaches the top of the escalator, he has already cut across Connecticut Avenue. He's made it to the median, anxious for what looks like his destination: a bookstore and cafe across the street.

She prepares herself: Dupont Circle. She was just getting used to the idea of the suburbs. She hadn't figured on Mr. Cates living here, where the rents are high and there are more White folks than Brown. *Samuel Cates can't live here,* she thinks.

Perhaps he is meeting someone, a friend or lover. In all the years that she's imagined him in her mind, she has never thought of Mr. Cates in love. It's only now she realizes that for a long time he's lived in her as sexless, much as she has come to think of herself.

She can't remember the last time she was sitting across the table from a date, worried over whether to talk politics, crack jokes, or make eyes. She can't remember. Can't or doesn't? Won't or chooses not to? *Too many trifling men in Washington,* she thinks. She's used that one many times, responding to co-workers or the busybodies at church, just before or after she reminds the nosy or concerned how many more women there are in D.C. than men. When she hears, *girl, you so right,* she breathes the pressure out and doesn't worry herself with how long it's been since she last imagined a man in her bed.

But she's envisioned men in many other ways: in the store, wandering the aisles in search of the mysterious products their dead mothers or ex-wives had used to clean and feed them; in the office, bullshitting their way out of casework; on the train, sly grin, furtive eyes over the Sports section and moist, scowling lips when she doesn't smile back. Everton Fox, the portly BBC weatherman, makes her smile with his four-button suits and the gallant sweep of his hand as it passes over typhoons in Australasia; his accent lilts what she imagines as East London, but she is sure she can hear the hint of his Jamaican ancestors' creole.

It troubles her that she has no image of what Mr. Cates finds attractive in a lover. All she can picture now is what she sees: blazer, khakis, running shoes, now nervously jaywalking Connecticut Avenue. She pauses, takes a breath, heads for the crosswalk, and prepares to enter somewhere she's never been in the city she calls home.

Lynette's mother told her husband to call Leena Morris, from down the hall, for her to help Mrs. Simmons help Mr. Cates. When Lynette would see Miss Morris on the elevator, Miss Morris would tell Lynette to call her Leena, even though Lynette's mother had told Lynette to say Miss Morris. Leena wasn't like Lynette's mother or Berthine or Odessa or anyone Lynette knew. Berthine wore her best hats only to church and managed to carry her two hundred seventy pounds on four-inch heels but still she called Leena Morris *one of them new-style women*.

Leena Morris worked late, but no one ever talked about what she did for work. On early summer mornings, when Lynette and her mother sometimes walked over to Sixteenth Street to meet her father halfway as he came from his security shift, she could see Leena's flickering, TV-blue living room windows, the only ones lit up in the building.

Months before Samuel Cates jumped, Lynette had been eavesdropping from the living room couch as her mother and Berthine talked in the kitchen about Mr. Cates: Sammy Cates, who only came to church on Christmas Eve and left early; Sammy Cates, up at all hours of the night; Sammy Cates, who spent too much time by himself.

While the two women spoke, Lynette was imagining Mr. Cates sitting alone in his apartment, maybe looking out the window, maybe looking into the alley. She tried to picture her mother, alone, sitting with a can of club soda at the kitchen table. Or her father, without his wife, sitting in front of the TV, no food on the table, no ball game on, no nothing going on.

When Leena knocked on the front door and slipped in, Lynette could see the get-the-hell-out-my-house look on her father's face. He waved toward the deck and told Leena, "They out there." Mr. Simmons was irritated by this—all these people in his home, from down the street, down the hall, through his roof—and him having no say in it.

Leena nodded to Berthine and Odessa and shot a wink to Lynette before stepping to the deck, and sliding the door closed behind her. Mr. Cates stumbled to get up, but Lynette's mother held him where he sat. She smiled at Leena, pointed inside, and without much more talk, came into the living room and went straight for the bathroom to get gauze and alcohol.

Out on the deck, Mr. Cates eased back in his chair. Leena already had his shirt open to wipe away blood and see if he was cut anywhere else.

Lynette remembers that when Berthine said, "She don't waste no time, do she?" her little girl's mind thought it was thinking what Berthine was thinking, even though she didn't yet know what that was all about. Berthine said to no one in particular, "I could say something but I won't," but pulled Odessa close to whisper something Lynette could not hear anyway.

In the café section of the bookstore, Lynette is on her second coffee. Mr. Cates is nursing his first. He's been at a table by himself since he came in, looking from the bar of the café to the front of the bookstore.

Lynette drifted in a moment or so after, orbited the New Arrivals table, and wandered into the front room of the café, which is also lined with books. She worked her way carefully through the Poetry section, tracing her fingers from *Z* on back before easing down to the table where she now sips at her coffee.

Samuel Cates hunches over his cup, looks to the street, looks into the restaurant at the back of the café, then back into his coffee. The track lighting warms the room, and in a glow that looks like late-autumn daylight, his features soften. The light shines on the skin of his head, where she had imagined the hair to be thicker. His awkward lean onto the table looks more like a habit his body has learned. His hands hold the cup like a chalice and he looks around the room with the same keen fascination she sees in the elderly who watch children at play in the park.

This is not a place Samuel Cates knows well, but he enjoys it, the jazz over the speakers, people speaking and laughing loudly, engrossed in the witty things they are saying. For just a moment Lynette watches a small grin flash on Mr. Cates's face, and then it is gone. Perhaps because he is alone or because she now sees how he's aged, he seems more pitiful. She is not sure why, but Lynette starts to feel that the lines in his face have come from more smiles than frowns. Just as Lynette comes to feeling this, Mr. Cates slips a small nip-size bottle of Scotch out of his blazer pocket and quickly pours all of it into his cup, which he shields with his arm from no one in particular.

The small bottle vanishes, and she marvels at the deft movement of his hands. Without a beat, he is back to his hunch over the table. She is thinking on wanting a little taste, too, something hidden, something quick and secret, maybe Scotch, maybe rum. She wonders what takes the edge off, the liquor itself or the secret of it, snuck into a coffee cup in a room full of people. Maybe both. She wants to ask him, *how long you been at that, Samuel Cates? You go to work sauced or is it just at the end of the day? That what gets you home?* But somehow she knows it's just a taste, every now and then. Sammy Cates, with his little taste on Connecticut Avenue. *All this time, where you been?*

Leena Morris had been on the deck with Mr. Cates for some time, the two of them talking as if nothing had happened. Mr. Cates seemed to have cracked a joke, because Leena was laughing. When she smiled, her mouth opened wide, and Lynette could see her teeth, which weren't very white, but they were set straight and apart from each other so that when she smiled she had a warm inviting face. She was moving her hands around as she spoke. Her fingers were long and thin. She moved them gently, like she was gently brushing away smoke, and Lynette was thinking that Mr. Cates must be watching that, too. Those hands, gliding through the air. The sun was bright on her cheekbones and her wide, flat nose. She was beautiful.

Lynette noticed that her mother was now standing at the sliding door holding alcohol, also watching Mr. Cates and Leena. And it was then that Lynette realized that everybody—

her mother, Berthine, Uncle Norman, and even her father—was watching Leena and Mr. Cates. Everyone watched them through the sliding-glass door and no one said a thing. The ball game was on. Lynette could hear it and nothing else. Mr. Cates and Leena both turned to see everyone in the living room looking out at them.

Berthine was the first to laugh. Mr. Cates was still smiling as everyone stepped outside. Uncle Norman was the last one on the deck and he was still laughing when he came out. He reached out to give Mr. Cates a beer, but when Mr. Cates took hold of it Norman held on, tugging it, then let go. Everyone laughed at that, too.

Then Norman said, "You a weird one, Sammy Cates. Next time you want a date, just call the sister; you don't got to be jumpin' off no building."

Lynette's mother stopped laughing. So did Leena. Everyone stiffened. No one would look at each other at first. Then Lynette looked at her father, who looked to the deck ceiling for a moment and then pulled Norman back inside.

Leena got up and hurried for the door.

Mrs. Simmons ran after her and shut the sliding door behind her. Before Berthine could say anything, Odessa pushed her inside. Lynette was left standing on the deck, alone with Mr. Cates.

Samuel Cates looked at Lynette. She smiled at him because she thought that he might too, but he looked dazed again. Once, as the elevator was approaching her floor, just for kicks, she said, *Hey, Sammy Cates!* instead of, *Hello, Mister Cates,* and that startled him. Her mother pinched her arm, and he turned back to face the door. She wondered what might happen if she got to talking to Mr. Cates. She put her hand on his shoulder. His body was rigid. Her mother had never allowed her to be alone with strangers, but her mother was off chasing Leena Morris, and here was Mr. Cates, left behind with her. Lynette thought about how she felt at recess, when it seemed that no one wanted to play with her; it's easier to be chosen than to ask.

"Hey, Sammy Cates," she said.

He had gauze in his hand. He was unraveling it and balling it back up. When he had several balls of bloody gauze he didn't know what to do with them.

Lynette put out her hand. "You can't pay no attention to Norman. He says stuff he has no business sayin'."

Mr. Cates shrugged his shoulders.

Lynette took a couple of the balls from his hands, which weren't very big, just a bit larger than her mother's.

There were two pigeons sitting on the balcony railing, and Lynette tossed the balls at them. The birds fluttered their wings and flew down into the alley. Mr. Cates watched this and squeezed the remaining gauze tightly in his hand.

"I think God makes some folks like Uncle Norman so that the rest of us can see what actin' a fool looks like." She reached to take the rest of the gauze out of his hands, and he closed his fingers around hers.

"I'm not much for all that God business," he said. His face was calm. If his eyes were closed he could have been asleep. He focused in on their hands. The tops of his were coarse, but his palms were smooth, and even though he didn't let go of her hands when Lynette pulled, he wasn't holding too tightly. If she pulled hard, she could have freed herself.

"You okay, Mister Cates?"

"You don't got to call me that." He loosened his hands.

Then Lynette did pull her hands away, and the gauze fell onto the deck. When she looked up the pigeons had come back.

Mr. Cates picked up the wadded cotton, stood up, and threw it at the pigeons. He threw the wads one at a time and missed wildly, but he threw them very hard. The birds flew off in all directions. Then he looked back to Lynette.

She suddenly wondered where everyone else had gone.

He went to the sliding door and opened it to leave.

"Hey."

He stopped and looked back at her.

"You not gonna do anything else crazy are you?"

He smiled and ran his small hand over the cut on his forehead. Then he gave a slight wave and closed the sliding door behind him. That was twenty-five years ago.

When Lynette slips back from this memory, Mr. Cates is gone. All that remains at his table is a ten-dollar bill under his coffee cup. She picks up her bag and walks to his table. The coffee is gone but he has left his faded Washington Bullets bag. It sits on the chair next to where he sat. She picks it up and runs for the door.

Lynette follows him a few blocks until she stops across the street from the building he enters, a retirement home in a renovated apartment building. Lynette can't help but smile, for this development fits her pity. She smiles and is immediately ashamed for imagining him as a drunk, senile man wandering the city, riding the metro, collecting meaningless items in an old bag lined with weeks-old newspaper. She stands on the corner, hand on the zipper of the bag, wondering if it will matter to him that she's looked inside it. The thought strikes her that what's in the bag might surprise her, telling her more than she wants to know. She stands under the streetlight, staring across the street.

It is a small building he has walked into. The upper floors have drop ceilings with large square light fixtures. Inside, the fluttering hints of shadows that fluorescent lights barely reveal. From outside the glass door, the lobby looks small. A hallway leading into the back of the building, a long table just inside the door, a few chairs opposite the table. He must be missing the bag, she's thinking, and how long can she stand on a dark corner, in Dupont Circle, NorthWest Washington, D.C.?

Lynette crosses the street, rushes in the door, heads for the hallway. There must be a resident directory near the elevator.

"Excuse me, sister. *Excuse* me!"

Lynette turns to see a large woman at the table she's just passed.

"Can I help you?" The woman wears the white blouse, skirt, hose, and shoes that nurses wear. She's got what is left of a sandwich in one hand, some other part of it in her mouth. She moves the food from one side of her mouth to the other. "You can't come in here, unannounced and all. Who you tryin' to see?"

Lynette steps up to the desk. She sees a registration book next to the woman's neat stack of *Jet* magazines. She runs her finger down the visitor's log. She looks down the hall, then points to where *S. Cates* is scribbled in the log.

"Junior or Senior? Junior just gone up. You from the drugstore?

Lynette is quiet for a moment, sets down her bag, holds on to Mr. Cates's bag. She feels herself getting nervous, unsure of what she knows.

"Senior been waiting on his pills all day. Man call down here four times, askin' after them pills."

Lynette starts to fill her name into the register.

"If you from the drugstore, I know Cates Junior wants to talk to you. And, Lord, take his daddy those pills!"

"I can wait for him down here."

"Wait on *who*? Cates Junior? He'll be up there another forty-five minutes! Sign in and get them pills up there. Been waitin' on you, girl. I don't want to hear no more from that old man tonight!"

Lynette picks up her bags. *I'm not from the drugstore.* She is not sure if she has said this or thought it. A panic fills her because she's run out of things to say. She is not from the drugstore, she is not visiting, she has had nothing to say before she walked in. Suddenly she loses sight of what Mr. Cates looks like. All of this is so far beyond what she had considered. Her mind flashes on a faceless, formless man sitting impatiently next to the bed of his father. The both of them are silent, one beside himself with waiting, his octogenarian expectation of the medicine's delivery eating at him worse than his need for taking it; the other, the son, anxious for this hour's visit to be up, thinking more about another Scotch in his coffee than anything else. Or maybe their life is nothing like this.

This is what bothers Lynette. She worries that the Cates, Senior and Junior, may be right now laughing about fishing trips and Momma Cates's collard greens or ribbing each other over dominoes. Maybe their life is like this, not stolid and monotonous, neither of them bitter at the other for something that could not be explained. And she'd rather not ask the nurse *and how's Senior doing?*, like some close family friend making small talk, because she hasn't figured on this other Cates, and a bit of socializing might get the nurse talking—and the nurse is the sort who talks—about how good it is that Sammy Cates comes to see his father: *Junior, he in here once, twice a week in the evening, once on the weekends, in for just an hour, and then he gone till next time. You could time the trains on that man.* And a talker like that will get around to some unsolicited reflection. *Lord knows we all could spend more time with family. I'm more bad than good with that, but, girl, I'm tryin'* . . . *You got family?* And then Lynette would have to answer, bag in each hand—groceries and unknown—weighing the answer: *yes, girl, I tell my kids the same, we got to get over to see their grands* . . . but she has no pictures of children when the nurse wants to see—the talkers always want to see pictures. So Lynette ponders: *no, my parents passed a while back, when I was in my twenties. Don't have any kids—no man on the scene—but if I did have children* . . .

Lynette grabs up her bag to leave. She will go back home. No train this time. If she's lucky, a cab will stop. She's just a zone or so a way, so it won't cost that much. She will go home, soak beans for tomorrow, take a bath, fix a drink, watch the news—just like any other night. But she's still holding this Washington Bullets bag, with no idea what's in it, and she's not sure what to think of this Mr. Cates if she doesn't open it.

She's halfway out the door.

"Hey, girl, hold on! Just hold tight."

Lynette sits in a chair, sets down her bag.

"You all right? If you want to wait, then wait."

Lynette looks at the wall past the nurse, then down the hall to the elevators, then back to the wall. She thinks of her parents. She's struck by how little they have lived in her since they passed. They are buried in the suburbs, at a place where the gravestones lie flat, so that the cemetery lawn looks more like a golf course. A place with few trees, but it was where she could afford. She has hung their pictures on the walls of her apartment, but it strikes her that she can't remember the last time she looked at them. She has not been to the cemetery in years—no reason, no explanation behind it.

Lynette thinks of how her mother had been with Mr. Cates the day he jumped through the roof of their deck, and tries to imagine herself doting on Mr. Cates in his elder years as her mother doted on Mr. Cates then. She imagines going to visit Mr. Cates on a Sunday in whatever retirement home he will end up in. Or she would drive Mr. Cates to church when his legs won't carry him to the Metro. Lynette would have called him the Friday before, as she would have done for years. She would help him down the stairs in such a way that he feels he is doing it himself, all the while asking him about the heat in his apartment, the health of his cats, how he liked the casserole she brought the week before.

As Lynette Simmons stares into the wall, she tells herself that she will wait for Samuel Cates to come down. He will be rushing out, looking for his bag. Maybe he will have forgotten. Maybe she will say hello as she gives it to him. She smiles at the thought of saying, *hey, Sammy Cates!* but instead she thinks she'll catch up slowly: *How you, Mister Cates? I'm Lynette, Avis Simmons's daughter, from way back. Meridian Towers Apartments. You remember me? I saw you on the train. We used to live in the same building, a long while back.*

The nurse has given up on her sandwich and looks at Lynette with a sideways glance. "I can call up to Mister Cates. You want me to call him?"

"No, thank you," Lynette says, then she eases further back into the chair and rests her bag on the floor. She thinks to say, *you don't have to call him, he's expecting me,* but instead smiles when she realizes that there is no need.

Crusade

for Jerome, father, friend, exemplar

Donald Biggers is working. Almost. He has just been fired. He waits in the foyer of a building when his supervisor has told him to go home. He is waiting to speak to his supervisor's boss, who won't be back until later. Every ten minutes or so someone enters or exits the building—a colleague, a doctor, a maintenance worker, or a stranger Donald had been hired to serve. They walk by without turning to smile or nod or at least to issue a flat, customary hello as they pass between the outer and inner doors of the foyer.

Earlier in the day, Donald counted at least twenty-three people who approached him directly with such cordial hellos, but that was just as people were introducing themselves over coffee, when fatigue was more familiar than names and faces. Donald had anticipated several more days of hellos, each coffee break more congenial than the last. But this afternoon, only two people have acknowledged Donald in the foyer.

Though he can't imagine how so many people could know so quickly that he has been fired, he feels that these passersby saw it coming—and now that he has been fired, why bother to

take notice anymore of this Donald Biggers, with his head of
unruly salt-and-pepper curls and unsettling stare that belies
the subdued register of his voice when he begins a conversation? There have been too many times when Donald has felt
this sort of dismissal. Over the years he has come to recognize
the shallow impact his assertions make in meetings or the way
he veers from the center of activity as he enters a room of people. Just now, sitting in this foyer, he does not know what to
do next, but he tells himself today will be different.

Donald feels he deserves the respect of a better explanation
than he has been given by the man who fired him. If Donald
is going to be fired, he wants it coming from as close to the top
as they will let him go. He's worked enough years to know he
deserves that much. Unlike most of his colleagues, Donald is
not young, but of retirement age, and though he is certain that
they know better, the supervisors on his latest job call him
Donnie, an assumed endearment he quietly despises.

He is actually past retirement. The pension from a career in
public service doesn't cover his bills, so now he works as a
standby disaster reservist for the Federal Emergency Management Agency. Donald's FEMA team walks a tight line of service, providing assistance to victims who file insurance claims,
running seminars to help communities organize against the
chaos and panic that follow disaster, helping people get assistance from other agencies. And there has been the hard part:
guiding without political agenda, assisting without advocacy.
Donald got on the reservists list a year before the World Trade
Center was attacked. Before the attacks, he had worked three
natural-disaster sites, mainly assisting with insurance claims

and organizing resources for the victims who came to FEMA for assistance.

After the attacks, he has been assigned to teaching disaster-site workers and victims how to help without letting local race relations and social politics get in the way of providing assistance. His supervisors have told him that his job is to guide people to help, not take them up as a cause. He has always found this difficult. Donald knows that the focus of their work provides little time to consider what is difficult for standby reservists. His colleagues and supervisors, all of them younger than he, seem uninterested in his concerns. This seems necessary for the work they must do, so he has found a way to think of them as more driven than aloof, but when he is sitting in his boxers on the edge of the bed at night, a fierce bitterness wells up in him and he leans into the angry sleep of men who have smiled through too many decades of service.

Right now Donald is not thinking about younger supervisors, low 401K yields, respect gained and lost. Sitting in this foyer, fired for the first time in his life, Donald is thinking of deep water, an easy-rolling mass of it, not lush blue or flat green but a molten-glass blend of the two, what the world looks like through empty Coke bottles. Water larger than a lake or inlet but more intimate than the sea. The sort of luke-warm, amusement-park water imagined from childhood summers or, if you feel as Donald does at night when he sits in his boxers, the sort of water you think about slipping under and not coming back.

In these late years, which really aren't old years for Donald—just late, because there seems so little left with which to fill the years—he finds that the thought of water eases his bitterness. When his attention has drifted during senseless meetings, it is that water he's nearly slipped under. Supervisors call him back. *Donnie, Donnie, you daydreaming about nineteen sixty-three again?* He will resurface, scan the room, notice that no one but Wes, a supervisor, seems terribly interested in his disinterest. Donald will give him a calm, cold, call-me-Donald-not-Donnie glare and make doodling look like keen note- taking for the rest of the meeting. Donald or Donnie, the name isn't as important as the years, all those hard years before retirement, years Wes hasn't lived: years in the Army, graduate school in social work, Peace Corps, and thirty years as an NAACP executive. All of that life building itself up to now: Uneasy retirement after the titles and political status. A pittance for pension. Government reservist employee. No salary.

When a disaster area was declared in some state, he'd fly in with a team that would operate there for a few weeks. The last time it was rural California in the wake of wildfires. By the time his team arrived, much of the flame had passed, but the sweet, raw essence of scorched red cedar hung on the stilled air. Other FEMA teams served food, distributed blankets, and co-ordinated with health-care volunteers. Donald's team was there only to assist with insurance claims and disaster-subsidy forms and to route people waiting in long lines to appropriate support services, but it was hard to explain the limitations of what he could do for people who had nothing but soot caked into the scowl lines of their faces and children who would hack up ash for months.

One man kept yelling from the middle of a line, *who do we go to get to help we can goddamn use!* Most were quiet, stunned, but they were all uneasy—all feeling the same helpless rage. They stood in line because they could think of nothing better, but they didn't want to spend their time filling out forms or be routed anywhere. They wanted extra cans of baked beans, bottled water, cough suppressants for their children.

That was for the Red Cross, his team tried to explain. Donald didn't have canned goods and medicine to give. But the locals glared as if they hated the reservists for not being the enemy, something or someone touchable they could strike back at. In a time of crisis, no one's patience lasts for long. After their weeks were up, his team would be replaced with another team, but in California, two of his colleagues gave up their duties a week early. The focus at the disaster site is on the people who are recovering from crises, and the team is trained to bear it. Right now the crisis is in Texas.

There's been a flood. Roads washed out, homes submerged, drowned livestock adrift among septic waste; a world of rogue lakes and wild torrents; a murky, boundless river and the soiled remains of what it did not wrench away. And though he would not wish this trial upon anyone, he finds himself fascinated with all that water, more forceful than expected, violent and random, Biblical. Donald is no longer a religious man, but the apocalyptic sticks with him. His daydreaming takes him to big water, beyond reach of shore, his feet taunted by undertow.

He remembers warm, tropical water. He was perhaps a hundred yards from shore, just where the shallow plane of the beach dropped to a lower shelf of the Atlantic. This was a few years back—family vacation in Fort Lauderdale, the day before Thanksgiving. He had driven his sons and grandchildren to the beach. They were looking forward to a day collecting shells, reading a few pages from a novel, falling asleep, rereading what slumber made them forget, slurping at sliced mangoes they kept in a cooler. When the sun got to be too much they eased into the surf, where the colder currents from deep water washed just under the bathwater warmth of the shoals. His eldest son and he had waded out for some distance and before he realized it, they were far from shore. They had been facing the sea, eventually bounding from the sandy bottom to keep their heads above water, then toe tips brushing the bottom less and less, until finally they were treading. Every once in a while the waves would push their feet into sand. Donald eased back, face to the sky, his ears sometimes above water to catch the far-off laughter of children on the shore, and sometimes below the surface, where all was the whisper of tide brushing sand, into shore, and back out to sea. His son had drifted in much the same way, the waves slowly widening the distance between them. Every once in a while they would look up, wave to each other, shout something that couldn't be heard about the clarity of the water or the laughing gulls above, riding on sea-bound thermals.

At some point Donald found that the waves no longer pushed his feet to sand when he expected, and he noticed how he could not hear the voices of the children running along the beach. He'd dip under, toes looking for purchase, nothing, and swim his way back to the surface. Each time he tried, he found no sand, the surface seemed farther away, and the current seemed to tug at his waist. He no longer took notice of the laughing gulls or how there was a fierce band of pre-dusk violet where the sky met sea. He focused on the shore, which now seemed a blurred abstraction of what it was moments before. *I can't make it back,* he thought, and for a moment his stomach churned with fear and excitement. Donald motioned to his son, who waved back, laughing, out of earshot. When the next wave came, he dipped under again.

His daydreaming washes him back to the moment where Donald is still in Texas, sitting in a plastic chair. He sits in the foyer of a high school, between the exterior glass wall and doors of the building and the glass wall and doors leading inside. For the past hour, when he hasn't been daydreaming of water, he has been staring at a painting on the opposite wall: a cartoonish Indian, small body, Kewpie-Doll head, war paint, and obligatory feather; bread loaf–shaped moccasins; large, three-finger hands, exaggerated spearhead, and *Go Warriors!* in a speech balloon flowing from the oversize lips. He looks from the school mascot to the floor, a beige-and-brown–speckled, pea-gravel surface that paves the hallways of every public school Donald can remember.

He was flown in the night before, assigned to provide instruction on diversity issues in the disaster area. This work is nothing new for him, but he's been reminded by a training supervisor not to carry a social worker's advocacy role onto FEMA's site. He must remain objective, he's been told. Stephanie, the trainer, is a serious woman, younger than Donald, but old enough to know what sort of work he has done.

As much as he would like to, he can not disconnect the fact that Stephanie is Black from his impression of her, as if Black is the default description—not how tall, how she speaks, where she went to school, how many kids she has. This is a lazy slip of perception he finds most annoying in White people and, when he recognizes it, in himself. No one refers to the man who fired him as the *White* supervisor, but this Stephanie is the *Black* woman among the supervisors. When on the odd occasion at previous disaster sites she and Donald shared a lunch table or coffee-talk at break time, he braced himself against questions about why the Black folks hung together. Through most of his career he would be the one to explain this or, better, join a table of White people so that there would be no question at all. Now he simply looks around the room: White folks from New England sitting with other White folks from New England. White folks with cats or SUVs or kids in Pop Warner football bantering with others who have the same.

Besides, he feels very little connection to Stephanie. He has told himself that she operates with such callous objectivity to take the focus off her Blackness. *We're not here to represent anybody but FEMA,* she has told him, with no interest in discussing the value of his past career. *Donnie, leave that NAACP thing at the door.* After years of convincing people to act as passionate advocates for those who are unable to act, Donald welcomes this objectivity: Run the diversity sessions, get paid, go home in two weeks. This resignation is a long stretch from the years before retirement, when work was a mission fueled by subjectivity and passion beyond default descriptions. At times he is shocked that it feels this simple.

He felt this morning had gone smoothly. Before and after the coffee break of twenty-three hellos, he had moderated two sessions of weary-looking but attentive people. Two sessions of twenty adults, all White people. That's what he couldn't help noticing. They stared at him just as he remembered White folks staring at him fifteen years ago, when he spoke in low-income neighborhoods about renters' rights. It was not their choice to listen to this man, but no one else had come to help them. That was Tennessee, where city taxes and developers' rents were pushing the poor out of their neighborhoods. Now it's Texas, and a flood has done the pushing, but the Texans share the same numbed resignation: What they own is under-water. They had come to this room to find out how local gov-ernment would dole out relief funds. Donald was to explain how everyone—Whites, Blacks, Mexicans, well-off, working-class, and impoverished—must be considered. They must sit through all of that to find out what they could expect for themselves.

The session involved presentation, questions, answers, and brief informal discussion—the only portion of the session where Donald had been told free-flowing talk should occur. No big questions, no distressing exchanges; that's how FEMA wanted it. They listened and scribbled intently, politely; smiled silently during coffee breaks and talked quietly among themselves, people gathered by what they had lost. Donald drank his coffee alone.

Before lunch, Wes, his White supervisor, pulled him aside.

"Donnie, somebody has—something has come up."

Donald said nothing. It was not what Wes was saying, it was how he was saying it. The tone, the hand on his elbow, guiding Donald away from the line forming where lunch boxes were stacked on a table. His mind went back to several other times when a White person had ushered him in such a way. He wanted to remind Wes to call him Donald, as he had done before. The way Donald was raised, Wes should have called him Mr. Biggers. But Wes was not the sort of person to pay attention to such things. If the situation called for it, a man twenty-five years younger who gave Donald his proper respect could leave off the "Mister." If folks gave him his propers, he could even stand being called Donnie.

"We have a problem," Wes said.

Donald knew the *we* did not include anyone but him.

"This morning, in your session, what did you say about the president?"

"I didn't say anything about the president."

"Two people say you did," Wes said. "They wrote letters of complaint." He'd removed his hand from Donald's elbow; they were far enough away from anyone's sight for such a gesture to remain necessary. "Some people are upset. *Very* upset. Not the time for that, Donnie."

"What people?" Donald's memory went reeling back to the morning sessions, looking for his mistakes, slipups, ways to interpret what he had instructed as upsetting. His Peace Corps training told him not to look for fault, but miscommunication.

"You just can't talk about the president that way."

"What way?" And Donald was almost laughing, because, for a moment, he was not sure about whom Wes was talking: Was it another supervisor, a field coordinator, the head of a local bank, the head of FEMA? Was that the president he meant? Donald, over the span of his career, had held many titles as the head of NAACP's in different cities—director, executive director, president, CEO—more than once, one title had been confused for another. He was thinking of asking to whom Wes was referring. He watched Wes standing there, staring at Donald's left shoulder, rolling and unrolling a manila folder.

"Donnie, this is a disaster site. In this climate, with all that's been going on, you know—this flood and all, a *war* on—people are uptight. You can't go saying things like that." Wes looked away to people sitting along the hallway, backs against lockers, digging into their lunches. "You have upset these people."

Then it came to Donald. It was the second class, after the question-and-answer section, the time his supervisors had advised for brief discussion and, if necessary, an exchange of ideas. They were supposed to be talking about equal treatment in the disbursement of relief funds—which districts get them first, which companies are awarded rebuilding contracts—objective observations to subjectively charged issues. But, as was true in Tennessee, fifteen years ago, he discovered that what these Texans wanted, now that they had someone like Donald in the room, was the chance to ask questions that might explain what they had not thought through on their own: *Why are your people looting our stores? Why does the governor give your schools more money when we're just as poor? Washington's Backhoe and Heavy Equipment got a contract before Ratliff's Contracting. Ratliff has twice the machines and been around three times as long. Is that what your affirmative action is supposed to do?*

Donald had stuck to his job, dodging all but the last question, for that one seemed the most general, the most reasonable and, though he was supposed to think otherwise, the most emotionally charged. These were the moments he remembered that made the work worthwhile, like breaking up an argument before it became a knife fight in an alleyway or the pinpoint concision he would craft into a controversial press release for the sharks of the Washington, D.C., media pool. The grace and power of what felt genuine in that flash moment among all the spin-doctoring. His comment to the group was quick and efficient, and because he figured these people were more interested in lunch than in the subtleties of how he might answer, he didn't think long on his response. At the end of a career of carefully chosen words, and for all of his experience, Donald did not think it would take much thought to answer as he did.

Someone had asked if he thought affirmative action was a crutch to Blacks and unfair to Whites. He replied that it had helped everyone. Convinced that Donald had no satisfactory answer for them, some of the people in the room eased back into their chairs. But then, to add levity, Donald said that without affirmative action, President Bush would not have made it—*George W.'s not exactly prime Yale material*. This, he thought, would get a laugh from blue-collar folks who, Donald was sure, worked much harder for what they earned than the president ever had. No one laughed, but no one seemed riled. But his recollection of how they responded became clouded. He thought of bumper-sticker slogans and T-shirt rhetoric he had previously dismissed as part of all that superficial Lone Star State of allegiance—*Don't mess with Texas*. Now he was thinking it ran deeper than he had considered.

Recounting the class to Wes, Donald finally sighed, almost

with a laugh. "I may have made an observation about President Bush. I made the comment during open discussion. I wasn't trying to convince anyone of some fact. I'm sure somebody just took it the wrong way."

"You have caused disruption we don't need, not right now." Wes was lecturing at Donald's chin and ears and forehead, his hands and Oxford collar. "People have written complaints."

"What people? If you let me see the letters, I'll be glad to talk to them. I'll apologize. Good God, Wes, if I had thought somebody would be offended, I wouldn't have said a thing."

"Times like this, you can't talk about the president that way. You're not helping these people."

"What do you mean?"

But Wes had already walked off.

Donald stood there for a moment, not knowing what to do. People shuffled by with their food, a long hallway of tired families, victims with boxes of chips, apple juice, and cold-cut sandwiches. He raised his arms slightly and silently mouthed, *I'm sorry,* to everyone and no one in particular, and then took his place in line for a boxed lunch. When he noticed that his meal had a pack of cookies, he thought things would turn out for the better. It wasn't every day he got cookies.

But at the end of lunch Wes came back, this time with Stephanie. She didn't say a word, but shook or nodded her head as Wes explained to Donald that he had been relieved of his position. He was to leave the building, head to the hotel, pack his clothing. Arrangements would be made for his return flight home.

"Tolerance is low in these people, Donnie, they can't take

any more disruption and discord. In times like these, you are either a supporter or a disruptor."

Stephanie nodded her head.

Wes seemed emboldened by this. Donald wanted to shout, *Wes, she's backing you up because she knows you can do the same shit to her tomorrow!* That was the get-loud-nigger act that got you part of what you wanted but never the whole thing. Donald had come this far in his life without getting loud. Then again, he couldn't name anything he had that was whole.

Donald looked to Stephanie, and she glared back. It was that dissatisfied sister look, like Donald had done something that she would have to account for. *Damn, Donnie, now you messed up my shit.* It wasn't disgust or disdain, but disregard, an air of dismissal. Donald had seen that look often enough in recent years. In his last years with the NAACP, when he went to the national conventions and regional meetings, he had stopped reaching out his hand to the younger directors, whose suits and social work were too well tailored for the job at hand. They carried that just-got-a-new-car look and made quick top-to-bottom assessments of what suit he had on. They offered canned responses to anyone who might be listening—some *back-in-the-day* bullshit reverence—and brushed up to some other director. Donald was a career NAACP man, a senior director, one of the dinosaurs they spoke to as they passed by on their way to someone else. Sometime, five years or so before he knew it was time to give it up, he started to count the number of soft-grip handshakes the young execs gave him, and when he took to noticing that he was counting, he knew it was time to retire. It was the in-the-way feeling that layered onto him each meeting, each year. Time to step out of the way. There was not much to hold him back. His two sons had been out of school and living on the Coasts. It had been years since his wife passed, gone just as he was starting to look forward to retirement. It was just him and an apartment in the Midwest, stacks of unopened bills, and time-share bargains he would never buy into. He thought more and more about how to get out of the way.

He didn't want to do anything practical or reasonable like a somber retirement announcement and smiling through scores of pitiful compulsory farewells. Why not go out like Medgar Evers, shot dead on his front lawn? That was a way to go. But just before retirement, and much like now, his late-night thinking went mostly to Whitney Young, who drowned in Nigeria. That was better, lost in fast currents, where no one, White folks or Black, no politics or policy, picked you out, let you go, or passed you by. In the sea there was no in-the-way. He thought of Adam Clayton Powell often, who didn't drown off Bimini, but could have. Donald imagines that it came down to a choice: Drift away or fight to shore. He wanted to be remembered like that, taken by nothing but a situation of his own making or undoing.

This problem with Wes and Stephanie was not something to lose his calm over. He knew the outcome of such a run-in with mid-level supervisors: Donald would request to read the letters of complaint. Wes would refuse. Donald would suggest that he apologize to the individuals, all classes, colleagues, and supervisors. Wes would say that could not be done. Stephanie would nod in agreement. Donald would insist that he be given a warning, and that's when Stephanie would speak up—*Don-nie, you were warned when we took you on.*

Donald would get nothing whole and satisfying from them. It's this that turns the tiresome to bitterness. Donald can feel it rising up in him. *Thirty years I spent helping folks, Black and Brown and White, just like these Texans. Who works at anything that long anymore?* But none of the supervisors take notice of Peace Corps or the NAACP. All they see is this calm-voiced, tired-looking man. Satisfied that Donald had nothing further to say, Wes turned to leave, and Stephanie followed after she looked Donnie over and sucked at her teeth.

And that's when Donald thought to a couple of years back, when one of his first training sessions was spent watching the president address soldiers who were shipping out for Afghanistan. The supervisors stopped a training session to watch the TV, as they had done often and for long stretches of time over those months. Wes and Stephanie had been there, as caught up with the call to war as anyone in the room. The president was instructing the troops on defending beliefs and freedoms, bringing the evildoers to justice, dead or alive. The president was going on about how *America must draw a line in the sand. Either you are with us or against us.*

Donald had smiled through much of the speech. He found the president's material so close to what Donald remembered from matinee Westerns he saw as a boy. Hardly the rhetoric of King, Farmer, and Kennedy, who had roused his sense of duty as a young man. He held onto that smile and said nothing to his colleagues, so that no one might guess he was more enter-tained than inspired. But he lost his smile when the president promised that the coming battle would be a crusade against evil. At this soldiers went wild with applause. Donald expected that from them. But he thought of the two Sikhs who were put off the plane he rode to his training session. And of the people in the room with him, many applauding as if they were on the next battleship set to sail. Wes, *woo-wooing* like a dog, and Stephanie, nodding, waving her hand as if she was testifying in church.

A *crusade,* he thought, and he wanted to say something smart and sharp witted, like *so, this is our jihad,* but he caught himself, because it was a sensitive time, and tragedy had made the president popular. Besides, Donald had never thought of himself as the sort to stun a room with wit. It was not the attempt at satire that failed him so often, but his timing and presence, or his lack of it; no one expected such things from someone like Donald Biggers; if it came from him, it must be underhanded. Someone might mistake him as being bitterly political, partisan to the point of insensitivity, and here he was, newly hired into FEMA for a job that would cover what his pension could not.

Since he watched Wes and Stephanie walk away from firing him, he has not been thinking about the loss of two weeks' pay or his unexpected return flight and life at home— retirement-age days, some spent looking for work, others at the windows. Instead Donald considers the glass cube of a foyer in which he sits, how it separates him from the people in the building. Above, particle-board drop ceiling—Donald can see where a leak from the air-conditioning unit has formed a rust-ringed tumor that bulges from one of the panels. He can go through the outside doors, get in a cab, fly home, remain fired because of some Texan who dislikes his humor, or he can stay, stake his claim, and walk into the hall-ways where he should be working. Stay or go, he knows these people will feel the same way about him. He can feel their disdain, even if he can't see who it's coming from. That's the problem, he knows. You can't see hate until it's already nailed you. All he sees is fatigue, strain, and streaks where mud has been wiped from their pale, sallow skin.

They line the hallways, families camped out on Red Cross blankets and army cots. There are hundreds of people in these hallways. Their homes, apartments, farms, and cars washed away or lost to this new dominion of mud. These are the folks who rent more than own or own very little. They have nowhere to go.

Nearly all are White, what Donald's father would have called *crackers*. Though he has tried not to stare, from time to time he catches himself watching them through the glass wall of the foyer. He cranes his neck to scan the rows of people for someone he would like to find but will never identify. Some-where, one of these down-and-outs has reported Donald to a supervisor. *One of you hates me,* he thinks.

He corrects himself. It's not hate. His father might call it that: hate, no-good, *evil*. But Donald has worked too long to dismiss their rationale as that simple or recognizable. *Igno-rance,* he tells himself. You can't see that, either.

What to do next has come to him in a way he did not ex-pect: through a memory, from years ago in Fort Lauderdale. He remembers sliding under the water, wondering if he would return.

He had been treading water for some time, but his body had been more bulk than muscle for some years, and he sank quickly. He could feel his chest, shoulders, and fingertips slip from the water's sun-warmed surface. He sank so quickly that it seemed to him the cooler, darker, water was rising to meet him, and when his head dipped into that coolness, his skin bristled. He felt as if a cold, blue hand had reached into his chest and tightened on his heart.

Then the feeling released, and he opened his eyes to the water. The salt stung his eyes as he strained to look around. This water was not a world of molten Coke-bottle glass, as he had fantasized, but more like a brown-smeared, dimly lit blue gauze that had begun to cover his eyes. He looked above, where rays of light cut into the water. Just then, the same undertow that was carrying him out to sea churned whorls of sand up into the shafts of sunlight, so that Donald felt caught among beams of small sparks slicing into fiercely blue water. It was more beautiful than what he had imagined for himself.

Just then his feet hit bottom, and he sprang toward the light. He thought of his son, who by then must have looked Donald's way and noticed he was gone. As Donald remembers it now, he seemed to rise more slowly than he actually had. He was coming through all of that wave-churned sand lit up by sunlight. That stilled him inside, so much so that when he broke the surface of the water he wanted to slip under again.

Sure enough, his son had noticed him and was swimming his way. His son would help him to shore, pulling him closer to the beach with the surge of each incoming wave, then resting and treading water against the riptide that had been drawing him out all afternoon.

———

Donald sits in Texas, waiting on the boss. When he cares to look into the hallway, he sees every now and then a colleague or a disaster victim steal a look his way, to see if he is still there, and upon seeing him, quickly turn away. He is still there, this uncooperative man, sitting in the glass foyer. He is the light-skinned Black man with the quiet, measured voice, the sort that his supervisors have found easy to speak over. He does not get as loud or look as angry as other Black folks he knows. But he feels the anger that he knows scares the White people they confront.

He feels a fierce bolt of that anger and then he feels a calm. Just in the past few moments. He does not feel in the way or disruptive, but quite simply right in his mind, as eased and settled as when his son helped him onto a beach towel and he looked out to the sea they had just been in. Donald took in deep breaths of air, tasting the salt on the wind, saw where the band of pre-dusk violet had risen along the horizon, and thought, *I'll stay awhile.*

Potcake

for Jason

The dogs have chosen him. Just three months ago, their noise was only a distant clamor he would hear without stirring from half sleep. If he did stir, Carlos would wake to nothing but the night wind tearing at plantain fronds across the way, the echo of howling lost in breezes blowing across the island or the jumbled memory of a dream. He has been on this island a year now, and until the dogs started using the brush outside his place for their regular nighttime romp, Carlos was convinced that he had found the peace that he'd come here for.

Before moving to the Bahamas, Carlos knew there was far more to the country than the sand and seafronts of Nassau and Freeport. On one hung-over spring break morning of his senior year, he ventured out of downtown Nassau and spent the afternoon drinking beer and playing dominoes with fishermen in Gambier Village, far from where the hotels encouraged tourists to go. Two years later, he was living in Gambier.

He came back for the out-of-the-way peace of it. The sort of peace that smooths over the seams between the days and nights, so that any Tuesday can feel like Saturday, what happens this week no different from last week. There are days he wakes and cannot name the date or day. So many of them feel the same, punctuated only by slight variations.

Most mornings he wakes to the hushed rumbling of low-tide waves where his road becomes a ramp at the edge of the water. When he looks to the sea, the fishermen's rowboats are small slivers a half mile out, just past where waves break over the reef. The wind blows from the eastern end of the island; with it comes rain under full sun, the smell of boiled fish from breakfast tables, and the far cry of laughing gulls. Afternoons filled with fits of angry rainstorms and the hot sun that follows. Days with beer and stewed conch. Other days with conch salad or steamed grouper. After dusk, mockingbirds call from the brush and night jasmine wafts through his screen door. The best of his days here are indistinct and perfect.

But now Carlos thinks the dogs are preying on him. Some weeks ago the dogs got into his garbage cans, and they have been back every night since. What was once a distant echo is now late-night canine revelry in the brush around his yard. It's been like this for a month: tipping cans, tearing at refuse and themselves, chasing after rats and marsh crabs, fighting, fucking, howling into the early morning. In the States, he would have talked to his neighbors or called the pound. But this isn't the States.

Carlos stands behind his screen door, sips at a beer, waiting for the dogs to step into his yard. When he finishes, he will throw his bottle to scare them off.

"Big man, ey?" Ezrena teases from the bed, "you jus' finish bein' all up in my stuff, smackin' my ass an' all, and now you'se 'fraid somethin' in the brush?" and she chuckles herself back to dozing.

At first the dogs keep to the shadows. Just beyond the edge of his small lawn, sea grape bushes rattle with their frolic. Soon they are darting across the yard and back into the bushes, moonlight catching the dull shimmer of their coats. He can make out flashes of teeth as they snarl at each other or, as Carlos has come to feel over the past weeks, at him.

Sometimes Ezrena makes his supper while he sits on the porch to watch the sun dip into the ocean. Sometimes Carlos says things like "you a together lady" when she brings him another beer, walks back to stir the peas and rice. He feels relieved that Ezrena can cook for him and not think less of herself. She picks quiet, still moments, later in the evening, after sex or just when he thinks both will drift into sleep, to tell him what she does think about.

"You're a restless soul," she says.

"Why's that?"

"In the last two years you had six jobs, lived in five houses, in two different countries."

"Papa was a rollin stone . . ."

"You somebody's daddy, ey?"

"I better not be."

"That ain' no jokin matter, man."

"You worry I got a sweetheart, ey?" Carlos says, trying on his best Bahamian accent. But Ezrena sucks her teeth, and he leaves that alone. "All that stamina you got, I'm too tired to run after anybody else but you." He laughs, but she's not having it.

"You only been here a year, you know? You jus' like the Americans dem what does come off the ship for a day. Lounge on the beach, get your drink on, off to the Straw Market, shop for your rum, shop for your cigars, take picture in the surrey, take picture with the police dem in they white tunic, take picture of the barefoot chirren and then you gone!"

"I'm right here, baby. I'm not going anywhere for a while."

" 'For a while . . .' Lord, please, like you on the run. You on extended vacation."

He has nothing to say to this. He has a newly stamped visitor's visa, good for another six months. He's used two others to keep him here over the last year. When the first ran out, he had to fly back to the States for a couple of days in order to obtain a new visa upon his return. It is as easy as that for Americans, Brits, and Canadians. But without a proper work permit, they both know he is not supposed to be earning money here.

She was there the first day he came into the restaurant. He cracked some jokes, said something shady about having family out in Cat Island and moving back to Nassau after school in the States. She kept to polishing her glasses. The manager laughed at all his jokes. Ezrena was laughing, too. Carlos didn't know if they were laughing with him or at him, and he didn't care: He was washing dishes that night.

Carlos thinks that his best answer is to say that it's not he who decides how long he stays. It's the Ministry of Immigration that says he has six months.

But she's sharper than that. "Ain' no six months keep you out, man. You ain' some Haitian refugee, squattin' down in

Carmichael Road, hidin' from Immigration. You people come and go as you please."

Carlos is reluctant to flush the dogs out. He has seen most of them bark viciously, only to cower when someone flinches at them. But the scars on children's hands and the occasional newspaper article about mauled tourists has kept Carlos watchful. Not every dog cowers. He stands behind the screen door, takes time to finish his beer before figuring out how to face off with them.

Ezrena rouses again and laughs from bed. "You more 'fraid of woman than potcake!"

He smiles at this and steps out onto the porch. Here they call strays *potcakes*—lean-bodied, anxious-eyed, mix of Lab, mix of pit bull, mix of a hundred breeds, loud as blue tick hounds, smart as poodles, wily like dingoes—the best and worst blend of what's left at the bottom of the stewpot. On hot days they lie so still that Carlos often mistakes them for dead. On cooler days, they chase cars and one another, packs terrorizing the lone potcakes who can't find a corner to claim. On some streets it seems as if there's a dog for every yard or, since Carlos has learned that few Bahamians claim ownership for the wild ones, a potcake for every set of trash cans. At night they run in packs, frantically hungry, horny, and sleepless.

Carlos has been on New Providence Island a year now, long enough to know the seasons, but he has to remind himself that in Nassau there is no winter like he knows: There is rainy sea-

son after dry season, the one hot, the other warm. Winter is
warm here. So he shouldn't worry over what he remembers of
last year's winter: frost on the windows, wind turning rain to
needles, and the frozen body of a dead dog that lay for more
than a month on a quiet block down the street.

That was Brooklyn, 1997, when he worked as a dishwasher
after college and everyone—even he, privately—wondered
how the hell washing dishes was going to cover the loans he
took out to pay for a degree he had yet to use. He moved from
a dishwashing wage, weed-smoking, post-college year in Ohio
to his uncle's apartment in Crown Heights, where he did much
of the same through the winter of ninety-seven. When he tired
of sleeping on his uncle's couch, he dishwashed and weed-
smoked a year away with college friends in Boston. He saved
enough tips to buy a ticket to the Bahamas, the farthest place
from the United States his savings would allow. When he saw
the *Bahamas?!* in the subject line of e-mails from friends he
would reply that the water was bluer and the people browner.

He moved into the first place he saw: a small cottage, stuck
in among other cottages of the Gambier settlement on the
western end of the island. One bedroom efficiency, kitchen, fur-
nished with bed, small table, two chairs, one dresser. The
dresser holds two pairs of long pants, jeans and slacks, a few
T-shirts, three guayaberas, a half dozen shorts. He hangs his two
work uniforms in the bathroom. The boots and leather coat that
were his cold-weather armor are growing mold under his bed.

Ezrena is a couple of years younger than Carlos but has looked
after herself since she was fourteen. She's a sharp-minded

woman, sharper than Carlos—they both know it—but Carlos went sucker for the sashay of her hips and the lilting cadence in her voice. Even after they've been sleeping together for months, she still teases him with the same flirtatious mock formality she uses to warm the tourists into bigger tips.

"So you call yourself Carlos?"

"Carlos Stubbs."

"Why your last name ain' Martinez, Ruiz, something like that?"

" 'Cause my pop's name is Stubbs."

"So why your name Carlos?"

" 'Cause my moms didn't like Charles, Junior."

" 'Bredder Carlos . . .' 'Li'l Cee . . .' What happen if I call you 'Carlito'?"

He is hooked. Carlos loves that she's smarter than she sounds—she can spin the Queen's English better than he can, but she saves that for her college courses and the cruise ship tourists. A hand on her hip, a long press-on nail pointing out his put-on bravado with her sassy Bahamian Creole. *Sexy,* is what he thinks. *Typical,* is what any past girlfriend would have said. But he's lived in the Bahamas long enough, he feels, to ease the suspicion that he is sprung on Ezrena's accent and ass more than on her. This is a cliché he is sure pricks at every American who gets his hands around the hips of a Bahamian woman.

When Carlos tells Neville, his across-the-way neighbor, about the dog in Brooklyln, he tells more part than whole. He leaves out the part about it being dead or frozen for weeks in the shade of a warehouse. When Carlos talks about that dog, he doesn't talk about the days when he kept his movements away from the windows because when he passed from living room to kitchen, the dog barked as if it lived for nothing else. Instead Carlos tries to get Neville laughing about the time he sat in the backyard of the apartment and smoked a cigarette while the dog barked at him from the other side of the chain link fence.

The voice that belonged to the foot that shoved the dog out the back door called the dog Candy. When Candy was put outside, it yelped back at moving shadows under the closed door, but when it heard Carlos's soft smoker's hack, the dog went straight for him and from its side of the fence let Carlos have it, a grating combination of yelping and barking for several minutes. The whites of Candy's crusty eyes were small rims pushed back by dulled, oblong irises. It yelped so intently that its body shook and it didn't bother with the saliva strung from nostril to chest hairs.

Suddenly the dog stopped, turned around, and trotted to a corner of its dirt lot to relieve itself. Carlos eased his elbows onto the back steps and watched the dog, watching him while it grunted out two Milkbone crumb–encrusted pieces of rage. Candy watched Carlos the whole time it strained to shake the last of what it couldn't shit. When it was done, it raked dirt with its hind paws, trotted back to Carlos, and picked up the barking where it had left off. That went on until Carlos decided to snub his smoke and go inside.

When he sees how Neville laughs at the story, Carlos doesn't talk about how often this happened, about how he seemed to be the only one in his building bothered by the dog's noise, about how he imagined feeding the dog rat poison, as the super had suggested one day. He leaves all that out, for fear that Neville will think less of him. Instead, Carlos tries to make the Candy ordeal funny, and Neville laughs at this story more than any other Carlos tells, real or imagined.

Neville has two dogs: There's Jobo, who loves Neville enough to play at home, eat the neighbors' dog's food, and shit on the lawn of the man two streets down, who, as Neville complains, "has he fat bank roll tuck in he pocket when he does play dominoes with the boys dem, but the whole time we's playin—t'ree hours we's play—he ain' drop nuttin' but a five spot!" And there's Sparky, who walks with the renegade limp of dogs who finally catch the car.

Neville manages dogs, his or anyone else's, with steak bones and whatever he finds to throw at them. "You ain' like no small dog, ey?" Neville is entertained with Carlos. "Youse a big, solid, steak-eatin' nigger," he says. "You should be shame, vex with some wingey-ass dog."

The potcakes are tearing through the sea grape bushes. Carlos can't see them from where he sits in a towel on his porch, but he hears them. Their howls have startled him from sleep, as if they had been barking inside a mix of dreams he was having about rabid collies and storm rain blowing sideways.

A few weeks back, when the dogs first kept Carlos up all night, he watched Ezrena while she slept, obviously less disturbed than he. She's lived her whole life in New Providence: a Grant's Town girl, used to the howl of dogs in the night. When she did stir, just enough to notice him out of bed and standing at the front screen door, she mumbled, "They just potcakes: full of foolishness. T'row a rock, an' they gone before rock done hit," and she slid back into sleep before he could ask her if she had ever thrown a rock at a dog.

In Brooklyn, he had thrown a brick at Candy. The dog had yelped, but dogs do that sometimes, like children who want someone to know they have fallen, so he feels better in thinking that maybe he had missed.

As often as he can manage, Carlos rides on the jitney bus Neville drives. When Carlos wakes up late, worrying about paying rent and his cable bill, he catches whichever bus comes first to take him to work. But when he cares less about being late, he waits on his porch for Neville, who always slows down and toots his horn to see if Carlos needs a ride.

When he's not worried about work, Carlos rides on three or four circuits of Neville's route. The jitney starts downtown, where he picks up the day cruise ship crowd, bound for beaches, or the tourists headed back to their hotels, out west. He has just installed a new air-conditioning compressor and has had the seats redone with a red-white-and-blue thick-band gingham. Each seat is covered in shrink-wrap plastic. "Tell me, bredder, who got seats like that?"

Carlos wonders if the colors are meant to make American tourists feel welcome. "American, British, French, Croatian, Bolivian—I ain checkin' for *that*," Neville says, "long as they money green, touris' dem can feel what they want."

In the past month Carlos has been jolted from sleep by the potcakes' early-morning howling, riding over the wind. It starts with one barking at a rat, the blue flicker of a TV inside a house, or nothing at all. Soon the dogs a few yards over have joined in, louder, more anxious than the first—some canine call-and-response meeting stabbing into the night. On and on, until the wind carries to Carlos's bed a screeching, wailing, deep-throat-growling mass of sound. On mornings after the wind has carried the howl of potcakes, he tells Ezrena that it's the wind that has kept him awake.

Shut up, Candy, shut up, Candy—this Carlos heard when the voice of the foot that pushed Candy outside wanted the dog to stop yelping from the pantry where it was put when it wasn't shoved into the yard. It got so that all Carlos heard on some early mornings was either *shut up, Candy*, or *shut up, Jervin*—Jervin was the small, sole child in a house of eight people, all over thirty-five. Sometimes Carlos watched Jervin playing in the backyard, doing his best to scare Candy. Jervin would be swinging a stick or kicking a flat basketball, shouting up into the air, *Shut up, Candy, shut up, Candy! You workin' my last nerve, Candy!* Candy pranced, darted around Jervin, stooped low on its front paws as if *Shut up, Candy* was part of a game the dog had been waiting all day to play.

When Carlos thinks about Ezrena, he sometimes worries that he is not worried enough about her. Is she happy? He can't say. Does she take him seriously? It sounds that way when she's upset with him. Is she satisfied when they have sex? He hopes so. Is he? He feels guilty for grinning at this. Recently, because she's been sleeping more, drinking less, and saving more tips than usual, he wonders, is she pregnant? No answer eases that one.

When Carlos thinks about Ezrena thinking about Carlos, he likes to imagine that she is just in it for a good time. That's easy to manage. Ezrena is a smart girl and she won't get hurt. She's been cheated on, been the other woman, suspects that for all Carlos's criticism about Bahamian men sleeping around on their wives, if he had the chance and wouldn't get caught, his answer probably wouldn't be no. He has reassured himself that since it was she who broke this suspicion down to him, she's not the sort to be brokenhearted.

They spend spare time at his place or driving to spots she likes to go. Sometimes they stop off at Nesbitt's for beer, steamed fish, and pool in the back room. On the rare night when most of the shit-talking pool crowd has gone home early, Carlos selects five dollars of slow jams on the jukebox and they dance in the dim light of the empty poolroom.

Most of the time she takes him somewhere they can be alone. He likes the quiet, and she has already gone through her party years, dancing with older men in clubs when she was sixteen. She takes him swimming in the bays east of Clifton Piers, where the molten-glass blue of the water is so rich Carlos swears he can feel it more than see it. Or she will fix them some drinks and drive him through the pine forests to the sandy beach roads in Adelaide, in the south. If the mosquitoes aren't too bad, they lie on the sand to watch the stars come out.

———

After he first discovered Candy dead, a block down the street, Carlos stopped to look at it every morning on his way to the train. He wasn't sure how he had missed it before. Candy lay in the doorway of an empty warehouse. It had been the get-on-your-last-nerve Pomeranian from next door. An overexcited, underloved dog that would bark at everything and nothing. Carlos figured that if the brick he threw did hit the dog, the thing must have run through a hole in its fence and died blocks away, along the shadow side of the street. Some time ago, before it left the Army Square Mall pet store, it used to have downy, sand-colored fur. Dead, its coat looked more like the oily-gray mat found outside the alley door of hotel kitchens.

Passing traffic was forever splashing gutter water along the building fronts, so the dog was glazed in layers of dirty ice. The body lay against where a steel rollaway door met the sidewalk, its glassy eyes fixed on the street, looking for the scrap that would never come. If Carlos could have ignored how the dog was frozen stiff, it looked like it might be resting against the door, as the Brooklyn strays often did to avoid the summer heat. After a week, Carlos could not rid his imagination of the person—the voice-of-the-foot, Jervin, somebody—who must be missing the dog. Carlos passed that dog every day on the way to his shit job. Every day he hoped that someone other than he would see the dog and take it away before the ice thawed. After a few weeks, he chose a different route to get to the train.

Sometimes Carlos stops in the middle of his shift and tries to manage what he believes is his guilt. If he is close to a break, he sneaks out the door and ponders his morality behind the latticework that separates him from the tourists at the bar. Lately, what he thinks is guilt stings him so randomly that, break or no, he stops, hand on the dishwashing machine lever, and waits for the feeling to draw near, sting, and then float away. His first defense is to mull over *what is there to worry about?* But that gets him thinking what all there is to worry about: the degree he is not using, the cigarettes he smokes too often, the woman he sleeps with but is nervous about loving, the way he put on the American-schooled–Bahamian act to get his job, and sometimes, among other things he left in the States, a dead dog in Brooklyn.

He has come to know his guilt well, so that it is not one large, bloblike mass he has to wade through, but more like several, different-sized blobs that drift both far from and near to him, sometimes floating away, sometimes flitting close enough to get him frantic. During Carlos's spring break trip, his first time in Nassau, he dove without looking into a mass of newly spawned jellyfish and thrashed in the water as if his life would end from an assault of small stings. His panic carried him farther from the boat, where his friends laughed at what they thought was a joke. Sometimes, when he wakes from nightmares about all that panic and no boat in sight, he thinks it is his guilt at work.

He tries to focus on the stillness, not the potcakes surely waiting among the sea grape leaves for him to go inside. When he had dozed off earlier, the night was full of more hushed noise than quiet. He woke to palm fronds rustling against each other and the far-off howl of dogs. All of that, muted by what he thought was the hurricane wind of a dream, barely made it to his ears.

But then the dogs were close, rustling through the brush like they were rooting out something they wanted. When they were close, near enough for him to hear their panting in the bushes, Carlos was sure that they were waiting for him to make a move.

When Carlos first started asking Ezrena to stay after work for drinks, he was drawn to how her hips looked in her waitress shorts. He was sure they were two sizes too small. Soon after, it was about how those hips felt when the shorts came off.

Now he thinks it's about the dip at her tailbone, tilt in the pelvis, the bones rising softly under the skin where the thighs rise one way to the hip and the other to what gets him horny. He loves the silence of the blue hours, his hand hovering on her hip, louver-split moonlight rippling across her ribs.

But that is when it seems she rouses and starts them into some discussion: *Why won't he wait tables instead of washing dishes? Did he see his ex when he flew back to the States to renew his visa? Why doesn't he ever ask about the classes she's taking? They could save money if they lived together in one of her auntie's apartments.*

When they get to talking about kids, she speaks like a woman who has thought out a plan but isn't pressed on using it. All the while his hand glides along her body, calf to thigh to the hollow where her collarbones meet. There are times when he finds his hands cupping her hip while she talks. Moments before, he would have just come in her or be riding that crest of sleep on the wake of sex. It is moments like these that he has grown to love and fear.

It is the moment yet to come that gets to him. Some days he thinks the next moment will find him gone, no interest in another visitor's visa, no more hand on her hip. Other days he sees his hand cupping her hip in every moment he looks forward to with Ezrena. Then there are nights when all he wants to think about is that hand on her waist—no thought of what happened before that moment, no what-happens-next— just now.

He focuses on that, hearing her speak but not really listening. When he says, "I love how articulate you are about what you are thinking," she turns to face him with a look he used to give bosses, professors, strangers in bars, White people who told him he was *articulate,* people he moved to the Bahamas to leave behind. He remembers how his response became a mantra, spoken calmly, sternly, tempered partly with pride and partly with the same look Ezrena's face holds when she says, "What did you expect?"

When the potcakes' noise wakes him he isn't sure at first if he is awake or asleep. In a dream he thought he was having, there was a wind like the wind of the past winters he had lived in the States, all of them gray and snowless, but fierce with cold and wet that froze where it struck. Cold wind from the flat farmlands of Ohio, where he moled through five years of college. In suburban Columbus, winter had been the persistence of wet cold and the fading of color—yellow-brown lawns, the gray skin of leaf rot clogging the culverts, the mottled trunks of sycamores, pale and sickly under winter moons. Carlos was student poor but lived with his housemates on a quiet lane of well-heeled families, where some people paid to fertilize their lawns year round.

Carlos thought his neighbors smiled to hide how much they feared him, living across the street. In his dreams, they all looked like Arianna Huffington and Bill O'Reilly: too much hair gel, too many handguns. They feared him and held pistols under their housecoats and Sunday papers. After he had lived for a few months in the Bahamas—just when he had almost forgotten about such dreams—he started seeing these people in the faces of tourists.

Carlos knew they figured him for a drug dealer instead of a college student: too many Black kids—there were three of them in a house of five guys—with nice cars parked in the driveway. Carlos felt sure the neighbors thought he was smoking pot all day, selling it to the other Black kids who drove up to smoke it with them and listen to music about smoking pot, killing police, and abusing women. Carlos was sure that the neighbors trained their dog to snap at his ankles when he rode by on his bike. That soft-eyed retriever on the corner would bare its teeth and heave at its chain to get at him. When he told his roommates about this, they said that maybe he felt that paranoid because he *did* smoke pot all day.

When he is startled from sleep, he is more in than outside of the dream he thought he was having: First it was all those Ohio winters, now it is just the potcakes, barking beyond the edge of the yard.

———

One of the afternoons Carlos decides to ride with Neville in his jitney, rather than go to work, Carlos is surprised to see an episode of *Lassie* on the TV Neville has bolted into the ceiling of the bus. *I drives and I entertains you,* Neville likes to say. The jitney is half full with tourists, heading back to hotels from beaches and shopping downtown. They are more disturbed at first by the volume of the TV. Some hold bottles of beer or plastic cocktail cups. All of them are red skinned from too much sun and drink. The men are sleepy eyed and beer sullen under their baseball caps. A couple of women laugh like schoolgirls at the cheap beads they have paid to have weaved into their plaited hair—something Carlos has noticed on tourists but not on the women who weave the hair, not on their children, not on any Bahamian the tourists assume would wear such a style. Soon, all of them, tourists and Carlos, are fixed on the TV.

As in every episode, Lassie is running to someone's aid. Some sandy-haired boy is scrambling frantically through trees and bushes that are meant to be brush but are situated artistically to shield where the hang of the backdrop meets the studio floor. The scene continues in a different shot locale. Lassie bounds gracefully over logs and stone walls to save the boy from the surprise cliff that is always waiting on the edge of the trail. When they meet, Lassie carries on with that familiar, measured bark and the boy interprets Lassie in full sentences. Neville is not watching, but interprets his own lines: "What?! Bredder Frank done fall and he all mash up? Where he is?!" Neville laughs, very entertained with his own theatrics. "Hol' on, gal, I comin'!"

When Carlos teases Neville about his video selection,

Neville tells him he has five or six tapes of *Lassie* episodes. "Lassie director used to live here, you know. Lassie done retire over to Lyford Cay, wit' Jaws an'—what he name? James Bond tingum from Scotland—Sean Connery an' de res' of de rich folks dem." Neville raises his voice and angles his head to the back of the bus so the tourists can hear. "Those four or five las' episodes, they done em right here." Neville knows them by heart, and Carlos is amused with how Neville gets the tourists laughing at his version of the drama. "Look here, boy, you turn Lassie loose or I show you how da lobster done get red!"

After a while Carlos catches himself laughing along with the tourists. When he catches himself he gets quiet and looks to the sea and then down at the checkered pants of his restaurant uniform. When Carlos looks up, he sees Neville is smiling at him.

"Yeah, Brooklyn, it a small world on Neville bus."

Carlos thinks that if he were to ask Neville what he meant, Neville would laugh it off, say he's just talking foolishness, but Carlos finds himself confused over whom to laugh with and what to laugh at. He stares at the pattern of his work pants until it is time to ask Neville to stop in front of the restaurant.

Carlos can still hear the dogs. He has stepped off the porch stairs and into the yard. He holds a beer bottle, now empty. He sets the bottle down and tightens the towel around his waist. The clouds have blown past his porch and the sky has turned out the stars. Wintertime, he's thinking, and here he is, walking the yard in a beach towel.

The dogs are closer now, in the brush at the end of the yard.

He can't see them yet, but he can sense them, six or seven rustling in sea grape bushes and among trash in the abandoned cottage on the lot next to his. They growl and bark in sharp, playful yelps, tearing apart what sounds like fabric. When Carlos makes his way through the bushes that separate the yards, he can see scattered contents of a garbage bag someone has tossed from a passing car. And there they are in the clearing of the abandoned lot, five walnut-colored and two caramel-brown, brindle-coated runts. All of them have small snouts and narrow eyes. They have been tearing at butcher paper and diapers; Carlos can smell the fish guts and baby shit. Goddamn potcakes, who Neville says will eat raw corn if they are desperate enough.

The brindles cease tugging at a diaper to bark at Carlos. They are loud and sound agitated. One charges him, snarling, teeth bared. Carlos doesn't move. He has watched this happen, potcakes snapping at Neville, at tourists who get too close, at children teasing them as Carlos rides past on the bus. The dog is almost at him, but Carlos is fed up. He stomps his foot. He has watched dogs dodge a kick, jump from cars swerving to hit them, cut around corners to escape a hurled bottle. The dog stops. The others have kept to their business, convinced that Carlos means them no harm. Carlos stomps again, and the dog scampers back a few feet, lets loose a string of nervous barks, which pricks casual notice from the others. Carlos wants to kick it in the ribs. If he could get close enough, he knows he would.

Just now he remembers back to Brooklyn: that brick, in his hand, then the brick out of his hand, sailing through the air, an angular object made round by its spinning after he had thrown it toward that little shit-dog, Candy. It had hit just short of the dog, which yelped as if it had been hit. Before it could set to barking back, Carlos lunged at it from his side of the fence. He took hold of the chainlink and shook it. Candy darted off through a hole in the fence on the other end of the yard.

He remembers how days before he had the brick in his hand, Carlos had made that hole. He used to think of putting rat poison in the scraps they set out for Candy, but decided the hole would be better. He had jumped the neighbor's fence and bent back a space just large enough for a small dog to get through should it want to get closer to any of the dozens of things it barked at outside of its own yard. And he waited for the dog to leave.

The hole happened days before the brick.

Days before the hole in the fence, Carlos had decided he could take no more of Candy. He had just stepped outside for a smoke. Though it was cold out, the neighbor's back door was open; steam from cooking billowed out. Candy was inside. He had just lit up when a foot shoved Candy out the back door, and the dog darted straight to Carlos, barking at him, it seemed, from the moment it was put outside.

"Can you call the dog back?" he had asked in a calm voice.

No answer, just Candy, barking. The neighbor's back door was open, and he could see shadows moving behind the screen door.

"Excuse me, could you come get your dog, please?"

But there was no response, nothing but Candy, who had worked up a decent amount of saliva on either side of its mouth.

"Can you call your dog?!" he shouted, thinking they could not hear him over Candy's noise, but before he could finish his sentence the voice that belonged to the foot that shoved Candy out screamed back, "Don't you raise your voice at me! Who the hell are you, raising your voice at me?!"

Carlos stamped out his cigarette. "Ain't that some shit," he mumbled to himself and went inside.

A day after the shouting and a few days before the hole, he happened to see a man sitting on the front stoop of the building where Candy lived. The man was short but thickly built, and he wore the brown uniform of a UPS driver. He was drinking from a bottle in a paper bag. Carlos had never seen the man, but figured that he lived there. He nodded to the man and started inside his uncle's place.

" 'Scuse me, brotherman," the man said and stood up.

Carlos walked to the bottom of the man's stoop and put out his hand to greet him, "What's up? Name's Carlos, I think you live with the dog who—"

The man threw his drink at Carlos's feet. "Don't you ever raise your voice to my mother, understand?"

Carlos was still smiling, not quite sure what was happening. Then he remembered, the shouting. "Oh, all that. Say, brother, I didn't know nobody was right there. It's your dog, brother. I was just trying to—"

"Say, '*brother*,' you talk like that again to my moms, and I'm gonna come at you harder than like I am right now, you feel me? I'm gonna come at you, son." He glared until Carlos looked away and then he turned to go inside.

As soon as Carlos sat down in his uncle's apartment, he

thought about rat poison. A few days later, he was jumping the fence to make the hole. A few days after that, when he threw the brick, the dog yelped and took off. That afternoon he sat outside in the brisk, newly silent air and smoked three cigarettes.

The potcake has stopped barking at him and stands in the scrub-grass lot. Carlos stands poised like a martial artist in a floral-print towel. The rest of the dogs have dragged their garbage into the the safety of the brush.

Carlos's mind drifts from the brick to the dead dog, frozen against the warehouse door. He began to imagine the dog, thawing as the days got warmer. On some mornings he thought of Jervin, missing Candy, the only thing he knew of smaller than himself in that house. Carlos imagined that Jervin cried after someone in the house told him that Candy wasn't coming back. Carlos imagined Jervin crying about that, not only because he was a lonely child, but also because he didn't realize he missed Candy until it was clear the dog was gone for good. When he thought of Jervin, Carlos figured the boy must have grown up quickly once Candy was gone. In Brooklyn it's important for a kid to wise up quickly—that's what he thinks as he stares down the potcake.

The brindle turns to join the others. Carlos watches, waits until they get back into their noise. He tightens his towel and turns to head back to his cottage. He picks up the empty bottle and tosses it toward where the potcakes carry on their romp. Carlos smiles, sure of a few things: that the bottle lands

without harming any of them, that they will be back tomorrow night and the next, and that he will lie down with Ezrena,
who could care less for what the damn dogs do.

Standing in the street he imagines her in the bed, how she
will turn to hold him as he slides under the sheet. He will
watch how she eases back to sleep, run a hand along her body,
and feel himself warm with the many nights he plans to spend
with her. He pauses on the porch before stepping inside.

He can see the moment coming, when he realizes his hand
has been on her hip a long while after returning to bed. Perhaps that moment will happen tomorrow. Perhaps it will happen years from now. Maybe it will be tonight.

He will be caught up in a haze between old guilt and new
confusion, because his mind will hit a junction—love, lust,
anxiety—all of it flashing in him at once. In the moment after
he lifts his hand and traces his thumb along the small of her
back he will think to himself that a few years ago he would
have done the same thing, noticed the small of her waist, flar-
ing wide into her hips, and he would have said, *baby, I love your
big brown-sugar behind*. But soon—perhaps days, perhaps years,
or maybe tonight—he will ease into bed and as he lets his
hand make that trip he will say, *if we have a kid, boy or girl, it
should have your name*. Part of him will be joking, but most of
him, nearly all of him, will not, and though he will feel at ease,
he will be surprised that it is he who has spoken in this way.

Rossonian Days

for Ernest Holliman, Earl McAdams, who carried the old way, and Nathanael Fareed Mahluli, who brings the new.

You hearing but you aint listening.

—MY NANA, DOROTHY HOLLIMAN

The memory of things gone is important to the jazz musician. Things like the old folks singing in the moonlight in the backyard on a hot night . . .

—DUKE ELLINGTON

Listen. This happens for just a moment. The car is headed north, to Denver. That's where the gig is. The band is from Kansas City. West by south, through Pueblo, and every dirty-snow mile of Route 87, stretching north by west. This kind of traveling never takes the short way. More road than anybody wants. Not much else to see. The fields will be gray for months. Land slips from the road, rolls in swells of rye and hay across the plain to the Front Range.

The car is long and the wheels are wide. Front grille stout like America itself. The car is a Lincoln, rides like horsehair across bass strings. No curves to this car, only rounded right angles—suggestion of flair, but nothing is small time here.

No two-tone paint job. All black. Six coats of pure gloss. Shine for days. Tinted glass. Chrome nothing more than nuance. More power switches than anybody will ever use: EZ drive *power* steering. *Power* windows. *Power* locks. *Power* antenna. *Power* seats. What don't got *power*, the car don't *need*. The whole deal—chrome trim sidewalls to suicide doors—holds more class than most will get from getting in. You don't drive it. *Ride* it. The Lincoln Continental four-door convertible: chariot for the *re*birth of the cool.

Inside, everybody's got room without anybody's last nerve being worked over. The bass is strapped to the roof; horns and drums packed like china; clothes for tonight rest on instrument cases. The worries ride up front, steaming the windows.

Call back to memories less rich but more grand, like Milt Hinton snapshots that didn't make print: Ellington, asleep in a cashmere topcoat, fedora brim angled across the bridge of his nose, head at rest on Strayhorn's shoulder. Missouri is outside. They glide through the dusk of the Midwest, "Lush Life" drifting on AM, night coming on.

In another image—maybe Ohio this time—Duke at work, writing in the small spot of a car lamp. Harry Carney sawing logs, shoulder to Duke's shoulder. Too many road gigs were cats filling a car like the last boxcar headed north: Sweet Pea, Monster, Snooky, all the rest, blessings on the stand, but all the same, smelly-sock brothers filling space where, if the Duke is on, a Black-and-Tan Fantasy is always birthing. Not all of his rides smooth, but you know the elders always wander the hard way first.

Call back to days of try. Edward Kennedy Ellington: Duke before there was Wayne, regent of a tight backseat, sounds making themselves on pages under dim light, no hambone room. Outside, it was always night, dark in the heartland, where brothers wasn't safe after dark. You ain't been blue 'til you had that Mood Indigo. Ride a million miles through Columbus, Des Moines, Peoria, Tulsa, Vidor, Lincoln, just to enter the Cotton Club through the front door. . . . Hambone, hambone, where you been?

Somebody before now played this road—someone heard by some or maybe never whispered—so drive this Lincoln like holding the family photographs, and when it rolls in, brother, stride right.

It is some time after the turn of the year: say it's 1965 or a year later, maybe years earlier. There's no stick to this moment, but it will echo. Don't need a year to know this story is old. The trip has been made by many: like making good time in a '31 Hudson from Baton Rouge to Chi-town. Been in moments like this, riding with hay discs strapped to the slatboards of a flatbed International Harvester bound for Macon. Been up to and down from Ft. Worth for a summer of Saturday nights. Skylark was the ride in those days. Chickory, pork chops, grits, a skillet of cornbread cooling in the pantry every morning. In and out of icehouses of all sorts, sometimes even those for *Whites Only*. Been asked back to and booed out of every juke joint on the Chitlin Circuit, southern route that splits the cats who are *down* from those who ain't, and *if you miss the A train, you have missed the quickest way to Harlem.*

No matter the year, it is winter. The plains are a hard, gray-brown bed nobody wants; there is the long road following the Front Range of the Rockies. For long breaths the road is lost in angry wind and tired snow, and the only thing that keeps the car on track is the tenor player at the wheel, working through Moody's "Tin Tin Deo," Afro-Latino jam, up from beneath the underdog's fatback jawbone. A downbeat thick like adobo sauce to go with that *arroz con pollo*; the band chanting . . . *oh, tin tin deo* . . . and now the conga is in it . . . *oh, tin tin deo* . . . cowbell, crisp like momma's catfish . . . *oh, tin tin deo, oh, tin tin deo* . . . a four-four swing gone East Harlem *bebop,* the rhythm something you know, but the rattle is new: stick on a can, good groove under the Lexington Avenue local, 104th Street.

Long after the tune leaves his humming, the tenor thinks he still hears it . . . *oh, tin tin deo* . . . on his last breath, from the backseat, deep in somebody's chest or fifty miles back. Wind keeps rhythm. White sky stained gray like old bone. The fields empty. More snow coming. Bourbon is passed from backseat to front, and somebody says if there's a God out in all of that, he best be blowin' for us. Then all is quiet.

Not much to say once you hear the call. A body has been waiting a long time for that call, through the passage of centuries, through all the rent-party nights and ten-cent coffee hours. Time was when days were three shifts: Some of one spent sleeping and practicing, most of two spent working or looking for work. Word spreads down the Sante Fe line, an ad cut from the *Kansas City Call,* letter from a cousin in Pueblo, an auntie in the parlor with the phone pressed to the radio: a "jazz-endorsed" P.S.A. from W-VBA, the disc jockey calling out from far away, late night, low and steady, like a talking drum across the bend of the savannah's horizon:

> *Are there any musicians left out there? Here's this from the Rossonian Auditorium, Denver's best kept secret: Management would like to remind you there's always a stage for great talent at the Rossonian. Maybe you have got a talent that we would want to showcase. Perhaps you're the next swinging sensation, ready to strike it big back East. Go East, young man, but swing in the West! Give us a call—Albion six eight six seven—tell us your name and address and let us know what your talent is: horn, piano, vocals? Have you got a band? Call soon, Albion six eight six seven, or write us, Management, The Rossonian Auditorium, two six four zero Welton, Denver, Colorado. Tell us what you can do . . .*

Many places are right for moments like this, but the moments are fewer than the places. Where it's at is now: the band, the car, the road, and where all three will stop. Kansas City is gone for now. The gig is at The Rossonian. In Denver. On Five Points. Where Welton meets Washington. Come night, the people are there, roasting ribs and frying catfish, domino games in front rooms, Cadillacs angled to the curbs like Chris-crafts. Five Points, where it has been and is. It's not Beale Street or 18th and Vine, but it wants to be.

The Saturday-night local headliner is bound to pack it

tighter than the mickeys allow anyplace else. Nobody has a care, except for showing up and showing out their hard-earned, store-bought clothes, ones that won't do Sunday morning, but do it right on Saturday night. Can't roll up to *that* scene in some small-money ride. Nobody will take the scene for serious. These days, cats are pulling out their best jive; everybody who's nobody is hustlin'. *Everybody can blow a horn, son, but what can you do?* So drive the Points in the soft-top Lincoln Continental *convertible,* shag top shiny in a stingy man's winter. Drive up in some sorry vehicle, that's what folks remember.

They remember Andy Kirk and Mary Lou Williams—*when you hear the saxes ride, what's the thing that makes them glide? It's the lady who swings the band!* Basie and Jimmy Rushing. They remember Charlie Parker. But Bird didn't need no car to break out of K.C. Mary and Andy floated in style through the West with the Twelve Clouds of Joy. And Elders are quick to say *ain't nobody worth a damn come out of Missouri since the thirties . . .*

But it is 1960, give or take some years back or forward, and the arrangement of players doesn't matter—a piano man, tenor and trumpet players, drums, double-bass man, maybe a trombone, maybe a singer—no one knows their names.

> *It doesn't matter, but everything matters: Bebop has died, Straight-Ahead Jazz is dying. The small traveling band ain't long for this road. Long-playing records play the hits—what's popular spinning on records for less than any five-piece group driving state to state. They not gonna like you out west because*

*you Sonny Rollins, son, they gonna like you 'cause they heard
your record was on the tops of the Billboard and Down Beat
lists. Or maybe you got an angle: Dave Brubeck and Chet
Baker blowin' Blues like the brothers, but their Blues ain't
about paying the bills. Only a few will rise off the highways
and land on wax.*

Make that no nevermind. *This* car is headed for a gig. There
are highways full of these long, black cars, carrying the best
jazz nobody's ever heard. To hear it *live*: another breakdown
chorus, Basie swinging "April in Paris" *"one more time . . ."* a
third reprise, volta, groove—call it what you want, it swings
just the same—*"jus' one more, once . . ."*

Music from the marrow. At clubs a rung above juke joint;
velvet-draped lounge or speakeasy; intimate auditorium, back-
lit in blue. No need for a name, just a love for Blues, a four-
four swing tapping your toe—*hit that jive, jack, put it in your
pocket til I get back. The show*: Standards spill like laughter, one
into the next; the piano man is running through "Twinkle
Toes"; the tenor is just sitting down; the trumpet man sips on
his sour mash and picks lint from his sleeve; the drummer's
got a new suit: Ivy-League cut, iridescent green rust shimmers
when his brushes ease across the snare, left stick teasing the
cymbal like a pastor's blessing. Late night makes early morning, the glow of early morning shows through the skylight,
stars like embers through the wire glass. A third set beginning, lights low, dim footers set brown skin glowing. Folks
look younger than they ever have or ever will.

*Play on, Brother, play on, it don't matter that tomorrow is
a workday or a Sunday or another sack o' woe day, play on,
because right now everything is right.*

No record or radio catches that. But it's hits that are selling
now, not that *better-get-it-in-your-soul* music, all its mothers and
fathers sold off to new owners. It's the sixties. Just forty years
gone since they lynched 617 in three months. Red Summer's
strange fruit rots slowly in our gut. We get silent. We learn
the ulcers we bear. Or we forget. But you know the Emmett
Till Blues. Where's your singing now? Just a whistle get
you dead.

*This is a voice stowed in the Middle Passage. Call looking
for Response. After the chain and yoke, there were weeks of dark
quiet, the wash of seawater against the ship's bow. Inside, a
song of rot breathing head to foot, row over row. This was a
voice that sang Benin, Ibo, Fang, Hausa. This is a voice that
learned Georgia, Louisiana, Tennessee, South Carolina, all the
Dixon below Mason. This is a voice that learned cotton, tobacco,
and sugarcane. This is a voice that almost unlearned itself.*

*No more drums, no elders' words. They beat you if you speak
out or refuse the labor. They hunt you when you run. They listen for the bell welded around your neck, smell you out with
hounds when you run from the noose. Not much music in hose
spray or last snap of rope, jolt of cord and spine; that razor
quick like fire and fierce between the legs. No voice in that
night.*

But Coltrane preaches "Alabama," so listen: People been hanging from trees; Elders gone north and west and back again; Harlem, Detroit, Chicago, burnt: northern lights when they told you only Mississippi was burning. And who sang the Oklahoma Blues? Tulsa, 1921: that fire fierce but silenced. No news carried that. That's our death, people: no story, no wire, no radio, no voice, no ear, no report, no Call and Response to know that people out here are living and dying. Nobody to sing their Blues. Nobody to hear it wail.

Listen. You got to listen: 'Trane's Blues. Four girls, baptized with bombs. Bessie Smith, a story we forgot. The ghost whistle of Emmett Till cups the street corner of every young Black man's dreams. People going broke on northern city Blues, and their voice, only thing they ever owned for sure, sold for the price of a record.

Soon enough, they don't want to hear no "Strange Fruit." Sing us "Body and Soul," Billie, they cheer. Smile and sweat through "Body and Soul" for the money thing. Soon enough, change chimes in Brothers' pants pockets as they easy step the sunny side of Lenox Avenue; Billie Holliday all but gone, another echo in the alley.

The road and the soundless miles are for the singers and players, heard and unheard. They all want the voice; they travel. Once they've heard the voice it will never leave them alone. They travel. Most will never hear it, but they travel. This is the road jazz folk play. Have played. Been playing. Been played by. Will play for.

I let a song go out of my heart
It was the sweetest melody
I know I lost heaven,
'cause you were the song

Before King's English. Before written word, there was story, in song and wail, drumbeat, hambone, and sandshoe, the hot breath of mothers birthing field-to-factory generations. Thick and light, the sound moved as the people did, on to East St. Louis, on to South Detroit and Cleveland, to Chi-town, where Brothers blew that hard, Midway city, get-ol'-man-Hawk-out-my-draws bop.

On north and east, to Philly, and of course the City, the Village, 52nd Street, and 125th Street, Harlem, Mecca at Lenox Ave, nothing small in Small's Paradise, where anybody on the move was moving. On out westward: Austin, Lincoln, Denver, K.C.—all the gigs before, in between, and after—all the way out to the Pacific, that high-tone, low-key, California-here-we-come land of give up the gravy.

Just one night, one good jam in Denver—tear up the Rossonian—and the skate to the West Coast was smooth.

After that, return to the South slow and easy, like nobody's
ancestors ever left it. A stroll on Beale. Cakewalk down
Rampart.
After that, leave it, freer than any freedom train headed
north.
After that, to The City. The road will lead to The City.
After that, only Ancestors and Elders know . . .

Some kind of way, the trip will be made. There are so many cities, all too far from Kansas City, but the trip will be made. Phone rings, the gig is on. Denver. The Rossonian. Down in Five Points. The Rossonian: two sets, one night, a hundred heads, five-spot to get in, two drinks to stay, a quarter take of the door. Fill the place—management is happy, band is happy, and like that, the Rudy Van Gelder is the call from Englewood Cliffs, just across the Hudson, where the studio is still buzzing from when Miles Davis's Quintet was the Word.

So the trip will be made: three days, two nights. Head out Route 24 after a half day's shift, roll past Topeka, already lit in the winter early dusk of the Plains, pass through Kandorado as the blue bowl of late night pours its last stars across the West; make Pueblo for the late set at the Blossom Heath. Two encores milk gas money for the trip—*nice work if you can get it*. Sleep off last night's drunk until just before new day's dark, then a biscuit, coffee, corn liquor, junk, or smack. Here comes Denver. The Rossonian: oasis in jazz nowhere on the way to jazz somewhere. Someday soon, stompin' at The Savoy.

And after the gig is swung, tired or no, never mind hangover, no time for a strung-out morning, the Lincoln will make fast back to Kansas City, the small low-money gigs, the stormy Monday job, the life that always expects the empty-handed return.

So the phone rings, for the bassist, the drummer, the singer, the piano man; maybe a vibraphone player—but maybe they ain't ready for the vibes out in the Mile High, not yet, and this ain't the time for testing new waters.

The phone rings for the horn players—the sax, trumpet,

trombone, whichever horns, any of them are waiting for that
phone to ring. Everybody wants that *taste,* like what Cannonball and Nat got on the grill out in California. Monk fixing on
which suit coat to wear—dark or light—while the car is running and the photographer is waiting. Ain't we all been waiting for *that* phone to ring? Cannonball Adderley filling seats
like it was summer Bible school. Mercy, mercy, mercy. Dizzy
blowing that horn easy as waxing the Cadillac: L.A. smooth,
beret, goatee, horn-rims, and herringbone. Ivy-League cut
suit, fresh bed, dry martini, *salt peanuts, salt peanuts.*

*Go get some. Don't bring no soft sound. There are few chances,
one or two big moments. Many misses. The young cats, they got
good at hitting the target, notes all dressed up and in line, so
on top of technique, the soul got blowed out. They miss. Those
Brothers will rattle some walls with a few records, but come
five years, those cats are quiet, waiting on that phone. They
missed.*

*The phone didn't have to ring for Satchmo, who never
missed. Not Charlie, who was blessed with more jam than he
could jive. Not Bessie, who was hit enough to bring it back
black and blue—beautiful like that until she couldn't bring no
more. Not Prez or Johnnie, who didn't know what slow was.
Not Billy, who didn't know what "no" was and gave her soul
to encores and needles. Not Ella, who never knew an off note.
Not Milt, who gave "Bag's Groove" to the grooveless. Not
Chet, who gave to music and no one else. Not Nina, who got
more sugar in her bowl, her well-deep voice the middle of whatever best and worst day anybody ever lived through. Not even*

Clifford, who lived through one car wreck only to be taken in another before he was twenty-seven. Not even thirty yet, and he needed no phone to ring. He already swung with strings, just like Charlie Parker.

The phone rings for the rooftop and boiler-room players. The brother running scales on his lunch hour. Down by the riverside. With mute when it's late. A bus-ride hum. Not yet twenty, but a lifetime waiting on that phone. Sometimes it rings. They pick it up. They say yes. They travel.

The bag is packed, shirt's been pressed for weeks, instrument oiled, shoes shined—chamois across alligator pumps, matchstick to clean each wingtip hole. The savings is cracked—quarters and singles from days of pinching for days of playing. The landlord is dodged. Never mind the bills. The bossman is conned: . . . *you see, I just gotta see my Auntie Berthene, up over in Denver, else she likely to up and die fore this time next week.*

And somebody will always be left behind. A woman, a man, maybe large-eyed children, but somebody's left on the porch, in the day's first light. They wonder what makes *this* time the time when it's the *Big Time?* What makes it different from the last Big Time? St. Louis: gone for three days. Or Memphis: gone for a week and come back with half the world dragged out in between. Somebody will be left. Somebody is always left. But nobody will remember after the record deal is signed and the reel-to-reel is playing back "If I Were a Bell," take two. Gin gimlets all around. Someone will tell the story about Ben Webster trying out the tenor when the piano had no luck in it for him. *In a mellow tone* from that day on. It will feel like that; your story will be told down the ages. When that new sound comes, everyone will know the name on the album—bookings sticking at Birdland, Leonard Feather calling for a *Down Beat* feature—and nobody will never, ever be left alone again. Whoever it is that's left behind, that's the promise left on their lips as night air makes their embrace stiff.

Inside the Lincoln it's quiet cool. Nobody looks at anyone else. Snow's still coming. The sax player drives the car quietly now, changes and progressions silent secrets to an inner hum of his head. The drummer is almost asleep, slumped against the passenger window as he syncopates finger taps between the hushed beats of passing fenceposts. The trumpet player works a soft-scat to the high C he's never hit. The piano man has blank paper at the ready. The singer low-moans spirituals that got her through the ten-hour days of working somebody else's clothes against a washboard. *Joshua fit the battle of Jericho, Jericho, Jericho . . .*

. The bassist rubs a matchstick, pushing it to spark, pulling back before the rasp springs to fire. The car is full with the quiet of knowing. Some kind of way, they know some sound is going to roll up the highway and reclaim the song-breath of Blackfolk.

Each looks from the car, feeling like the voice isn't in the horn, or the hands, or the head, but lost somewhere out in this land and sky, *way out west,* vaulting farther than the road will go. Listen out there for the Call, dropped by some ancestor rushing west or north, when making music first felt like some step-and-fetch shuffle. Mommas wait years for a voice like this. Some fathers leave home looking for it and never come back.

This voice something like some thing drifting in the summer air of childhood days, caught and lost in sun-glare. It's wind lingering in the branches of the boabab just before rain covers the savannah. An Elder whispering. A mother's sigh carried on the wind, the rasp of callused hands across burlap bags when the cotton is high. It's Biloxi crickets, never seen but heard, in want of wet and hot, loud for days even in winter, through the cold, hard bright of day, out here, on the winter-bare spine of the Rockies—miles of dry and nothing—where crickets echo only in imagining.

The tight air waits for any sound, and when the bass player strikes his match, everyone is startled. Wait for it: brass stopper and snare skin, bass string strained, sevenths and discordant ninths sustained on the high registers of the ivories. *I let a song go out of my heart.* Nothing is captured: not time, rushing past the Lincoln, come and gone, down the road fast, like it's the car—not the passing of seconds or minutes—pushing the hours; not this vast rusted-out bowl of land spilling from the Rockies; not the wail of prairie birdsong, ringing like something forgotten, impossible in March, not here, not now, not this road.

I let a song go out of my heart
Believe me, darlin', when I say

I won't know sweet music,
until you return someday

The music of open air is waiting. The Blues has done its sliding, the Bebop's been straight and never narrow, and still here's that yearning, like the songs were so many grapes to be plucked and rolled around in the mouth. Driving from gig to gig, all fixed life loses itself for want of that fresh new groove. Everyone wants the sound we haven't heard yet. Since we were children we wanted that song to fit in somewhere between the first jumble of quarter note and half rest and the last few miles before the gig; measure after measure of notes. And that sound is taunting, take me in.

. . . child, take me in, roll me in your mouth, under your
hands; pull me from blank space and empty air and make me
beautiful: love me. Begin the Beguine. I am a Love Supreme. I
am the song you've always wanted, so love me.

It is hours before the Rossonian. Night has already covered Missouri. The wind and snow are dropping off, and it's near dusk in Colorado. Sun so low it lies sideways into the frost on the windows. The Rockies are all but gone, last light like a bright wick on Pikes Peak.

The Pueblo gig has been swung, is now only another last night, and this is the hour when all feels still; air cups the cold without wind, martins roost on the powerlines, and that long road from Kansas City is lost in the swirl of snow wake. All that road going, long and hard, not because the distance is great or the time is slow, but because the trip is not new.

There is no company but the crackle of prairie air across radio waves and a worry of what Denver holds in store: an old town, maybe a new night; fresh start, worn body; maybe a different crowd. The same women in different dresses, the men in their one good suit. Another night of promises never spoken. To the body: *Please, no more, no more up and down the road and in and out of the Blues*. To the people: *Tonight, on this one night, we truly are glad to be here*. To whoever was left last night: *You know I'm working all this for you, baby*. To the nameless body at the end of this night: *You know I'm working all this for you, baby*. To the bottle: *You know I'm working all this for you*. To the smack, the junk, the horse, the krik-krak monkey, five-and-dime-sho'-nuff-right-on-time-feeling, *you know I'm working all this for you*. The horn, the strings, to the drums, those piano keys, and the run that's coming tonight, it's gonna be tonight, it's *gotta* be tonight, because it needed to be tonight for the past five years, *you know I'm working all this for you*.

It takes the heart all day to find its beat for the big night. Soon as the gear is packed out of the Colorado Springs Club— even though there's a night to be had in the Springs—the hands start twitching with want for the next night. Where's that song? Waiting on a song to come: For all of the sound in the world, Colorado Springs the night before the Rossonian is a world of too much quiet. Soon it will be provin' time. Hands, be still.

Heart, be loud.

Denver will rise out of the plain. The road will soon pull the band down Colorado Boulevard, past homes where maids and yardmen work toward tonight. *Begin the Beguine.*

The streets will rush toward Five Points, a turn into the alley, the rise of stairs to stagedoor from the cobblestones. An open door and a taste of Rossonian air. Breathe once, let out the long road coming. Wait a moment. No breathing, in or out. The quiet room. Step to the empty stand.

Imagine walls lit from the floor. Imagine arched alcoves vaulting into a dome the color of any night full of lovers. Night in Tunisia. Imagine calls of the ancients, taking their rest above the balcony. Hear the drums, the voices. Somewhere voices call across grasslands. Imagine a room with doors all directions, not just north. Now inhale, take in the thick, dark air of from here to who knows what's next.

In one of those long-mile hours they wondered, *Why this long trip? Why have we gone all this way to have so little?* We have come this far, through many beginnings and endings, and rebirths, to this: No more to show than we had before we began. We been down this road, but what of this long life and no voice?

We "wonder as we wander," and maybe we make it big at the end of this moment we've been driving to. If we don't make

it, we'll steal away until we do, and if we do, we'll be play-
ing for the money and the name, but someday, somewhere down
this road, or the road to L.A. or the road to New York, some-
body's going to say, boy, you got to use the back door; boy, smile
that big-lip grin for the camera; boy, you real lucky to get even
ten percent of the take at the door . . .

Then we remember why the Call and Response die a bit each
day. When that happens, will we look out to the flat, barren
horizon, still voiceless like now, still driving to that next
chance, and cry, what craziness brought us here?

But anybody who's played up and down these roads will tell
you that something touched them sent them flowing, somebody spoke to them, dipped them in Call and Response.

It could have been Basie, or Big Joe Turner, shouting the
Blues down Vine Street, "Kansas City Blues" swung in a low
key, "Black-and-Tan Fantasy," or havin' it bad and that ain't
being good, but it didn't have to be. The sound that says
play me came before mouth to mouthpiece or stick to high
hat.

It was Momma singing "Get Away Jordan" in the back-
yard or it was a frontroom evening full of her momma's stories.

It was Daddy's comin-home whistle and Sunday-stroll scrape
of wingtips on porch steps.

*It was the late-night laughter of an uncle back home from
Up South, on the road, looking for one night's meal and one
good year of work.*

It was a grade-school teacher, short on smiles, long on the
blackboard screech and scratch sharp through the chalk haze
and radiator knock.

It was the wind-heavy sigh before summer storms.

The early-evening call of the Icee man in mid-July, a joyful
echo gone too soon after childhood.

*A reverend at an all-Sunday service full of Tennessee heat.
Every spiritual almost forgotten. Every low bellow. Each high
wail of every Elder come and gone. It was somebody testifyin'.
Like a whole tentful of folks bearing witness in the middle of
some South Carolina field.*

Getting ready to take the stand, one of these musicians will
tingle with a remembrance of childhood and fantasy afternoons. And of long Sundays. The Rossonian audience will remember Sundays, too. Right then, before the blowing begins,
something mighty spiritual will happen. *Come Sunday.*
Whether it's song or sermon, or both being the same, the peo-

ple will come from the offices, the factories, the markets, and the fields, where song and sermon were born. All will remember how that reverend had it together: everybody's story in one Sunday afternoon.

And that rememberance feels like taking the stand.

It will be hot like the August of '23; only Elders speak of that. The congregation has waited all day for the sermon. Men's Sunday-white collars ringed with sweat; talcum the women dusted above their bosoms gone in that first hour, when the organist broke into "Old Landmark."

Children have dozed, stirred, and fallen off again to the heat of high summer. Tithe plate's been passed around enough so that everybody's given, even the one deacon who's passed more plates than he ever helped fill. The choir's turned itself out, rising from "In the Upper Room" to "He Saved My Soul," and now, after the sun has pushed its dust-heavy beams from the back of the church to the front, they are tired. Everybody's tired. Been tired since before last Sunday. Since before the church was built, burnt, and rebuilt. Before runaway prayer meetings. Before men came with Bible and whip. Been tired.

The Rossonian audience will be waiting. The band will soon be giving in to that next moment of happening. It's like that for the reverend, too, and as he steps to the stand, afternoon sun angles through the transoms, shafts of light burning on his lectern like a signal fire. He walks with the step of wise griot women. His brow is furrowed, his blood is quick. He smiles at young ones and nods to the Elders, and then starts in with *my brothers and sisters, we come too far to stop singin now . . .*

This is when stories mix: traveling band from far away taking the stand, hard-working people stepping out to be graced with music, and the air of that room many times graced itself. This could be Zion Baptist or Minton's, back in Kansas City. There's something to be heard. The Word will be played. This is the language many know but few can speak.

> *. . . a Love Supreme, a Love Supreme, a Love Supreme, a Love Supreme, a Love Supreme, a Love Supreme, a Love Supreme, a Love Supreme . . .*

Soon it will be time for you *to take the stand.* Time's come to blow, that's the real time, when the lights lose their glare, faces in the crowd spring from smoke-dark into the footlights; the band is in the groove, *sho' nuff,* but they sound mono while the jam that's buzzing in your head is all *stereo.* Hi-fi. Good-to-the-wood, down-to-the-wax groove. And you heard it from way off, like back into the bridge of the second song in the first set, when "Cherokee" was busted out like anybody who's somebody from Kansas City would swing it.

From way off, you wanted that groove, you heard the jam coming, like before anybody took the stand, before the Lincoln pulled to the Rossonian stage door, open like any drumming circle in a congo square, sanctuary from all roads long and tired, from the long way north and the width of the Midwest.

By the time you feel it, the jam has been at work from way back, *music back to your momma,* when hand slap and downbeat filled southern evenings, drums or *Weary Blues* cotton-picking song, rising into the heat-faded poplar and pollen-heavy pine that divided plantations; still farther, on the slow spine of the Blue Ridge or rippling above turtle wake in some South Carolina swamp, where many had run and few masters were greedy enough to follow. Back then and there, you might have heard drums and song drifting from the Dismal Swamp and the Big Thicket, places unlivable, but more livable than living chained with iron, with the bloody knuckle from cotton husk, with a new God and *His* words, with a hard-handed driver called silence.

To get here from there, remember the songs of Elders now gone. Take Duke's hand through the "Money Jungle." *Steal away, steal away,* follow Harriet Tubman from the swamp, from prayer meetings, from memories of tame and kalimba chime, follow Sojourner Truth on the railroad that runs only north and west, catch the train, it's Underground, it's straight ahead, the A Train, Coltrane's Blue Train, it's the only train, *follow the Drinking Gourd, follow the Drinking Gourd.*

And from there to here came the groove that fills your head. A sound that needs no reason to be, no story, no event, no particular year. Just the knowledge that somebody may be out there, just beyond where you begin to hear your song drift past hearing, out to where there's a brother or a sister in the audience, down the block, in the next state, on that next plantation plot; maybe nobody you love, but somebody who came from where your people came from, and with just an utterance there may be an answer back, like any *right-on, praise-the-lord-pass-the-peas, I-heard-that,* call-and-response, because out there, they know that yes:

> *this voice comes from somebody, and it tells the story of who I am, who my people are, day by day, and no matter joy or the weary Blues, I will lift my sound to the evening air—across tired miles, across rivers I've known, across the sea I never knew could bring so much dark to light, across the bones of my El-ders—because I know that somebody out there will hear it, nod their head, answer back, knowing the same pain, the same Middle Passage, many other passages from then to now, and can know a great many things, but need know only that this is a voice, it is blowing to the world, it is bold, it is strong, it knows no yoke, no money, no god, but knows a way. It is my language. It is the story. It pushes against the hard morning of yet another day, and it is mine. It is mine.*

Germinating

for Taylor Lynne

There was that time, that series of years, fifteen through seventeen, that passed in such a manner that it felt like one long, evolutionary drag of a time-ignorant year. I had been lucky then, or so I thought, through the time of thirteen and fourteen. Puberty had been kind. Not many pimples, no cracked voice, no incredibly frog-like legs. It seemed as if the flow of events in my family, the family itself, or the death of what youth lived in it, willed me to be older without much thought or feeling of the passage.

There was no anxiety, no interaction with girls, or should I have called them *women*? I can't remember what my mother called them. Maybe *ladies*? I felt nothing. For or against. To or from. They were just there, my father had me believe, like paintings, like distance, like my mother, or my great aunt, Lauralinda, and her territorial smile.

Nothing very eventful or strikingly different occurred until the year that was seventeen came along. There wasn't a new car to be excited about, or even a driver's license, but sometime

during a series of hot, dusty, columbine days in early June
there was that family reunion in Denver.

Some memories of my childhood are more vivid than
others, either vaulting into or escaping from the white space
of daydreams and the ghosts of rules I affirm or deny as having followed, gone against or forgotten. I envision scores and
columns of relatives in some of my daydreams, so many of
them are now left behind in the trapped time of that reunion;
others remain clearly distinct and alive, and a small few flit in
and out of my head like standard bearers to the army of my
most elusive memories.

What I often remember first is the dust and visible heat of
City Park and the weight of mile-high air on some of the older
relatives who sat under large oaks, trying to fan themselves
free of their breathlessness and discomfort. I remember relatives grouped by common names and similar smiles, but I also
remember never noticing so many different shades of brown
skin in one place. I remember there being too many people,
too large of a mass for me to receive any one part of them to
mark with lasting clarity beyond that day. Then I remember
that they are my family.

The folks migrated to that park in Denver much the same
way they had moved North and West drifting from the Post-
Reconstruction, traveling with a sense of promise and unhur-
ried urgency. They came slowly to Denver, as old people do: on
trains, not planes, driving reliable Chryslers and Chevys and
riding in back seats with pillows and magazines to ease the
wear of the long trek.

I was sitting on a concrete bench watching my relatives
who were holding paper plates of cold chicken and looking for

someone to embrace. My father sat next to me and told me what it was like to be them: old and still outliving the rest from year to year. A whole group, a whole parkful, an entire family, missing somebody to hold. I gave this some thought, but I was also doing my best to look indignant for having been forced to be there. My father's words rolled off me, and soon I was into my chicken, greasing my cheeks.

"Just like every child your age: sit and eat, tend to yourself . . . That better be the best chicken you ever ate, boy." The voice, from behind me, cut into my ears, and I lowered my plate to my lap. I turned around and rose.

"Ohhh, hello, Auntie Lin—I mean, Lauralinda." I hugged her small body. "I was so glad that you decided to come. I didn't think you would."

My great aunt, Lauralinda, who hated to be called Auntie Lin, stiffened slightly in my grasp and then broke free. She tried to appear as if she were looking for something in her purse. Her purse was very large. I thought to myself that it might be funny to ask her if it were meant to carry everything she had brought with her from California. But I looked at the rich, serious tone of her light brown face and knew that she wouldn't laugh.

In the shade of low branches, her posture avoided an easy guess of her age. She showed years, but I couldn't tell how many. My grandmother used to tell me that her sister liked to stand in the shade because it showed off the tone of her light caramel-rich skin without the haze to give it a yellowish appearance.

I stood there wondering what to say. Her face wore an expression that made me feel that she was about to say something, but she just looked at me. I was too young to realize it then, but I think that she had a way of making you speak to her first. A real "lady" would never speak first. I stood there, not knowing that it was meant for me to say something.

"Well, Lin, hah, have you tried the potato salad?" My father started in. "Ole Gail has done it up good again!" He ate while he spoke, alternating food with words and pocketing chunks of potato in his cheeks to enunciate what she craned to hear. "And how 'bout that chicken? Damn!"

I noticed that Aunt Lin had no plate to hold and she wrung her hands. She looked like she didn't want to be holding anything.

My father continued to eat, not paying attention to whether she answered or not.

"Hey Dad," I said, "I need some more Kool-Aid. You going over to the drinks?"

"Noooo sir! Chicken's too damn good! You got young legs, boy, get it yourself!"

We three stood there for a long moment, my father still eating. Aunt Lin and I watching him eat, both of us understanding the situation. She didn't say anything. She looked at my father and he stopped eating. I figured that she must have practiced a long time to get that expression, and it must have been one that I was raised to recognize, because it made me want to leave. Then again, maybe it wasn't really that look, but instead my own uneasiness. I only knew the weight of her stare.

With a quiet voice made audible by the shakiness of it, she leaned to my father and gestured with her hand, "Roland, go get some beer."

And as if a lever had been pulled, my father went off in

search of the beer cooler. I watched him walk away, thinking how out of place he looked at this reunion: bright blue seersucker and red bow tie. He always had an appearance of forced change about him that led people to say, *well, my, Roland, you have changed . . . hair cut? lost weight?* Last year it was yellow pants and a green double-knit shirt.

Aunt Lin was looking straight ahead, her hand still half raised in the gesture that had sent my father off. She was looking at something far away in the rippling haze of heat beyond the shade of the oak trees.

"Your father . . ." She reached for something in her purse, "he isn't a bright man. Is he?" Her concern for wrecking whatever conception I had of my father was secondary to whatever was in the leather-looking vinyl bag that she carried like a baby. From her purse she pulled out a large lace handkerchief. The handkerchief was fine, perfect, and yet this moment was uneasy to me. The air, the mass of relatives, my father, Aunt Lin's strange pale-green hat, which I'd just noticed. I only had a feeling that I should say something. We looked funny, both silent, both still standing.

"Yeah . . . I mean, yes, Dad is sorta weird at times." Something better than that.

She caught my eyes before I could look away. "Weird? I didn't say *weird,* child." She flashed the cloth. "'Not bright' is what I was meaning. *Dim-witted,* understand?"

"Just s'pose it's that beer, Auntie. With that tie he does look kinda simple, though," I said it quickly and made an attempt for my neglected chicken.

"Son, some people *look* simple and some just *are.*" She seemed satisfied with herself and began to fold the kerchief into a neat triangle. She dabbed the cloth roughly around her lips, unknowingly removing bits of flaking makeup.

"Sit down," she told me.

And we sat. At that stage, I had begun to figure out the importance of conversations that I would have with adults by the tone of their voice when they told me to sit. Usually my mother was best at directing me; her powers of implication were phenomenal. It didn't take more than a very simple, quiet, *let's sit for a while.* Or sometimes it was just a look, like in a social setting where she could not rely on my ability to understand her spoken implications; she knew that look would land me. Something about *that* look. It was damn powerful. I can remember my father driving home drunk from an Orioles game explaining to me that it was important for women to have that look. He breathed it out in a half mumble and never explained why, but the thought intrigued me. After my father had set me off on that thinking, I considered myself an expert at tracking that look down. I was certain that my sister had grasped the notion of it by the time she was three, and I figured that my only defense was the ability to recognize it.

I looked at Aunt Lin for a long while. It was different with her; no implications. I remember she once said that *ladies* could be indirect when it was absolutely necessary, but otherwise it was frivolous; ladies who get what they want are direct. She studied the channels of fabric in her handkerchief. Very direct.

"You really shouldn't stare at old people," she said.

"Just noticing your hat." I told her it looked nice.

"Shouldn't lie either."

"Sorry."

"Shouldn't have to apologize all the time."

"Sor—Okay." We sat there for some time. I was watching my Uncle Jimmy from Milwaukee try to explain the rules of horseshoe-throwing to some second cousins when I heard my aunt sigh deeply. It was a breath that sounded more like fatigue then boredom. She took off her hat, set it in her lap, and began to poke at it with the hairpin that had held it there. Amazing. The youth of her hair. Her face. She looked at me with a curve to her mouth, and I thought she must have smiled like that when she was a child.

"It's an ugly hat." She looked to the horseshoe game. "I didn't have to worry about looking my best here. And besides—"

"Isn't that the hat that Ginny gave you?"

She turned to me quickly at the mention of my other great aunt.

"Yes."

Her sister, Ginny, had always been too flashy for Lauralinda's taste. Ginny carried clutches. Lauralinda had a purse. And she only wore a light foundation makeup to highlight her light brown skin. Ginny had proudly brandished red lips throughout her life.

I started to say sorry. While she watched the game, I looked at her hair, knotted up neatly, perfectly. It was too shiny, as if it were not her own. I could not help staring at it; I had never seen her without a hat outside of her house. All these years, hidden under hats and in the dim light of her home in San Diego, her hair had not aged. Barely any color was gone.

At that time, when privacy and mystery were everything to a boy my age, it seemed to me that the deep brown on her head was her best kept secret. I felt deeply satisfied in that.

"I wonder where your father has got off to." She began working to put her hat back on. She was just filling dead space, a true lady holding up her part of a conversation; I felt that she didn't really want an answer. I didn't want to reply.

She was still struggling with the hairpin. All I could do was watch her. *Shouldn't stare at old folks.* I reached to help, but she pulled away and quickly jabbed the pin into the hat on her head so that it stuck at an odd angle, like an antenna. I wanted to laugh. It was obvious that it was not as perfect as she would have wanted, but she had done it herself, without help. She didn't need to look for the mirror in her purse.

Across from us, the horseshoe folks had taken a break to grab a new batch of ribs off the grill. Someone yelled about getting some more pictures. Someone else hooted about getting more beer. They were good folks. They wore their best leisure clothes. Hugged each other. They laughed with their teeth showing.

Aunt Lin still faced the horseshoe poles. Her hands rubbed her thighs.

"You don't understand what's going on here, do you, child?" She watched the wind sweep the grass. She just sat there, waiting for me.

"Well, I don't know. There's a lot of people here I've never seen. I don't know them."

She sighed and clutched her purse.

"Good. That's . . . good." She turned to me and her face looked weakened. I thought she might cry, but she put the handkerchief to use and covered her face; somehow it prevented tears.

"That's very good in a way," she breathed. "It's really not

worth it. You're too young to know it, but these folks really don't matter. It seems like you can hug them all now, get to know them for a few days, but soon they'll leave. They'll be gone."

"Well, we can't always be together, Auntie," I laughed. "That'd have to be an awful big house if—"

"No." There was a slight wheeze in her voice, but then strength. "No. They will leave you."

"Auntie?"

"This is the last one of these damned things I'm coming to. It's not worth it. Spent a whole life getting away from these crazy people. And now you come back and they don't understand what's going on. Trifling Negroes. They're worthless. They just leave you. And it doesn't even matter; they never had any class anyhow." There was sweat at her temples, and she looked off towards some of the older relatives sitting near the drink table. "Soon they'll all be gone. Take your pictures now; only way they'll ever look like *somebody.*"

For a moment I lost the sense of where I was. All of those relatives seemed to be floating through the park, blending into and separating from one another, and the visions of those who were dead lurched out of a past that my parents had pressed on me. I could envision the mass of my family at some point dispersing and slipping from me as I grew older, carried away on silent waves. I imagined myself on some expanse of water, watching them drift to different bodies of land. There was Aunt Lin, sitting on a beach at sunrise, much like the beaches my grandmother had told me about, where they used to go as girls and look for sea shells. I envisioned Aunt Lin sitting on that beach holding her arms to her body as if their frailty might make them fall off. She had her face held high, not smiling, but also not frowning, not appearing to want much of anything more than what she had right then. She was looking into the sun. She was the only one on that beach.

"I don't like pictures all that much, Auntie," I said, feeling a need to breathe.

"Well you better start!" She seemed surprised at me, and I couldn't meet her gaze. Her voice came out clear and definite. "You'll come to care about them. You have to. You won't even want to; you'll reject them, but you can't get away from them."

I was hearing her, but I was also forming and editing a picture in my head of my mother, father, sister and me as the only passengers on some cruise ship just off the shore of the daydream beach where my aunt was. I wasn't sure where we were going. It felt like a long way away, though. And I couldn't swim.

"You don't like your mother, do you?"

"No, I do . . . I—"

"Or your father. It's all right. I figured you were lonely; that's why I came over. Not good to hate so much and be so lonely. Not yet, child."

We sat and stared at parallel horizons, each with our own focal point, but both out past the shade of the trees, the overflowing trashcans, the sand boxes of the horseshoe pits and even further, beyond even the near flawless green of the golf course. If we had been on a pier, we might have been looking at the same harbor entrance for different boats to arrive.

"You don't like *me* much, do you?" She didn't look at me.

"I—I don't know, Auntie."

"You better not. You're better off that way." She gave out another life-tired sigh. "Besides, you kids these days don't know how to treat a lady. Stare too much." And then she giggled like she had let out another secret.

I looked over to where most of the relatives were lining up to get ribs. I barely knew any of them. One man, my third cousin Clifford, was trying to take pictures, but he was standing against the sun, and the relatives were reluctant to get their photos taken. Finally, he took a few poor shots to satisfy himself that he could take them whenever he wanted, and put his camera down. I had the feeling that Aunt Lin was watching me watch cousin Clifford. I turned and met her eyes looking at me. Many things hit my head right then: the quality of anger that lies hidden between the known and the unknown, people who were cared for dearly, too much, not enough. Relatives lost and found. Drifting and forgotten. Alone.

And the thought of my aunt's hair, unraveled, in the dark, far away in San Diego, spread on some clean sheet for no one to see, not my grandmother nor even her other sister, Ginny, now dead. And the photographs that would come from this strange family reunion. Remembrances through eyes such as Clifford's. We looked at each other a long time, my Aunt Lauralinda and I. Shouldn't stare at old folks. I smiled. I tried to imagine the picture that we might make together.

"That really *is* a nice hat you've got, Auntie."

She eyed me, looking as if she meant to break the confidence of my compliment. I thought she might tell me to leave. But then her face softened, a hint of that young girl's secret smile.

She looked away for a moment and then back. Her fingers

were working the leather straps of her purse in the absence of something to hold. Maybe we both felt like hugging each other right then.

I got up slowly, not worrying about saying "sorry." I went off to get Aunt Lauralinda a plate of chicken, thinking how when I got back I would ask her about hunting for sea shells on the beach at sunrise, and she would take all afternoon to tell me. I would listen quietly, not bored nor bitter, sitting there with her, smiling.

Leaving the Dog, I Saw
a Buzzard in the Road

for Lenox, an old companion

Under lazy oaks and through pestering raindrops, I drove towards a farmhouse on a grassy hill in Georgia, my dog hanging his head out of the car the whole way there. I was taking him to the farm where he had been born. I was taking him there to live out the rest of his years. I couldn't tell if I was sad or just anxious to be done with it.

The ride was both slowly traveled and gone too quickly. The glare of the sun wore on us longer and longer between each grove of shade-giving oak, the hot, baked road, angry and immediate, vaulting us uncomfortably fast towards the promise of each rise where the road rippled in sweltering heat, lost between the asphalt and heavy sky. I focused on each horizon of wave-like heat out on the road, feeling drunk and weary with the weight of the moments to come. And the large black Lab in the back, his ignorant tail anxious only about where the car would finally stop.

———

It had taken minutes. Painful, that thought. We drove up a farm road scarred with ruts and stopped in front of the house. The scene became romantically, sickly obvious as if it were some stolen stroke from a Wyeth or Homer. A gray-haired man smiled from a window and signaled for us to wait while he came from upstairs.

While we waited, my dog and I walked the yard as two young lovers, each one waiting for the other to signify the parting. I had talked to him endless early mornings before, but now words seemed as inappropriate as me expecting him to lick my face one last time. I was not able to care for him properly anymore, and he was in need of so much, so much that even the immensity of this hill and farm and the whole of pastoral Georgia could not contain the instinctive love that he had been born to retrieve and need.

The man came out and smiled at me. He stooped to greet the dog, already rubbing him in his favorite places. I chose to leave quickly after that. As I took the dog bed out of the trunk, I could envision the place where it would sit: in a cozy pantry or next to the man's large rolltop desk. I gave my dog a last pat on the head. Then I rushed to leave, running from his anxious stance and the confused tilt his head always had those times that I drove away without him.

And driving from that farm, I put my hand constantly to my face. I could smell the last time that I rubbed under his neck. My hand had gathered the world of his being, hints of camomile petals and fresh mud from our last walk, the slight suggestion of sassafras and periwinkle hidden away in some fold of bushes or lost patch of wood that I could imagine with smell but never own with my eyes. I held my hand to my face for long stretches of time and wondered what new walks he would now take without me.

That voice was there, telling me I had done what seemed right, but then there was the buzzard, deliberate and slate-colored in the road as I crested a rise. I had to slow down and then swerve, for the bird's posture told me that it did not care what I valued in life. As I went by, it moved sluggishly out of the road as if its affinity to the passing on of life was stronger and more real than mine was able to be.

For a moment, I could envision my reflection in the dark bird's eye. I was vested as the perplexed missionary in the face of his ill-aimed parishioners or the lost child with a goldfish in his hands, realizing that the nature of people, animals, expanses of land and even air itself mock us bitterly and stab at our perception of owning anything that we really didn't create, but, instead, bought or took or were given. We ply our most anxious and confused actions with what we claim the best of intentions, but later, lost in cars on empty by-ways, we find ourselves burdened by those things we call ours, and those intentions slide deliberately away from us drifting slowly, knowingly off the road.

After a few miles, I stopped and tried to hold something of that day in: the green head of the hill, the weathered house crowning it, the patches of blight-wearied hemlocks, the fifteen drops of rain on my windshield, the smell of my hands. The bird.

I sat there, imagining that as I drove away from the farm and from the dog, I heard a gunshot or perhaps the loud crack

of a board on something like bones. I imagined that I heard
something violent that somehow made me sit more comfort-
ably, as if, by fate, the steel-haired man had decided to kill the
dog and by striking it down, fulfilled my childish belief that
my ownership of him was the core of his existence and, with
our parting, he had no further purpose in living. Maybe I
heard this sharp fickle echo.

Or perhaps it was just the falling of a branch in the woods,
the screech of late July cicadas, or the gravel under the tires.

As the eye of the bird might have hinted, it was not a gunshot or a splintering board in the fullness of that north Georgia farm.

As I drove away, perhaps I heard some slight rasp of the
straining cord that breaks in all of us as we grow older and
come to understand how the ownership of things or people,
anything, is never what makes us live, but clearly marks how
painfully we all journey to the grave. I could look back down
the road, far off where it lowered and then rose again into dull
heat, and wonder where that buzzard was. I could even drive
back, come upon it, still in the road, and replay my swerving
over and over, turning the wheel less and less each time. Each
time hoping to connect with that bird, the sound that I was
still hoping to hear and the heat that was still pushing me to
move quickly away, always, always, away.

What's the one thing you hope any reader will take away from your story collection? Did you write with the intent to impart a specific message?

I want most for readers to witness how our lives and memories are swept up in the swirl of stories, those that we are told, that we remember, that we construct, that either form the way we have become or vibrate within the selves we are becoming.

This was a powerful directive for me as I was thinking about and writing stories over the last few years. Beyond that, I don't think I had a specific message that pushed my writing. I do know that there were particular moments and ideas to which I wanted to bear witness. Not to forget. That may be another important thing I'd like to share with readers and that may be hanging in the balance of many of the stories' conflicts.

What inspired you to write this collection?

With my first book of stories and with the writing of the first few stories in this collection, I don't think I knew that I was creating a set of stories that might work together. With the first one, I was influenced by so many styles and in many ways that that book looks like a sketchbook of narrative studies, not unlike that of a painting student who tries to figure out the ways of craft in the work of great artists. At some point those studies became the first collection of stories. I did not plan on the shape and thematic movement of the second collection, but after writing a few, I realized that the stories were guiding me to a particular creative space. The thing that solidified my thematic mission with the stories was the engagement of an assignment I sometimes give to students: take a story by an established writer that fascinates you, moves you with its content and/or craft, and set out to rewrite that story. Think of those art students you see in museums, trying to unlock the secrets of the great ones. I challenged myself to do this with one story. I have always been very taken by Sherwood Anderson's "Death in the Woods." I spent many years working through "In the Swamp" to get at what I think Anderson was getting at. It doesn't matter that the stories are not similar and I know I have not mastered what Anderson achieves, but in the process of meeting that challenge, I learned a great deal about the power of story within the narrator who tells it. On a larger scale, the whole book is in many ways my attempt to chase after one of the greatest collections of American short stories, *Elbow Room* by James Alan McPherson.

What are some of your favorite books and authors? Which writers have influenced your work?
Aside from James Alan McPherson, there are other writers and artists who guided my work on this book: Zora Neale Hurston's Harlem stories, Beth Nugent's *City of Boys*, James Salter's *Dusk,* the work of painter William H. Johnson and James VanDerZee's photographs, and, of course, too many jazz

artists to count, but McPherson is masterful in delivering. I've been moved by his work from before I knew that I loved writing fiction. In many ways, I hope in some humble way that parts of this book might honor the gift he has given the world; I hope it's a worthy response to a discussion he began.

When did you first know you were a writer?
That's always been difficult to answer. When I look back, if one's awareness of being fascinated with stories—the hearing, telling, sharing of it—is a large part of a writer's self-awareness, I discovered this as a very young child, but by no means did I recognize that as being connected to writing. I didn't start writing stories until college and didn't realize I was hooked on this craft until a few years after college. I did the MFA thing, worked on sending stories out, and was lucky enough to get my first collection published early on in my life, but throughout those formative experiences, I can't say I was aware of myself as a writer. I knew I loved to write, I knew it was a part of me, but if asked about what I do, I would have been more likely to name the job that paid my bills. Even in recent years I might tell folks that I am an educator or a coach before I tell them I am a writer. Some years back I read that Auden quote about a how a writer is a writer when writing, just as a bus driver is what a person is when driving that bus. I think I've come to feel it in that way: when I am thinking, working, or living in the writing life, then I am a writer, and this means that I'm coming into that knowledge in new ways everyday. Other days, I'm a teacher or coach, a man mowing the lawn, washing the dishes, or more often than not, a crazy person scrambling to pay his bills.

How does your upbringing influence your art?

I used to think I had that figured out, but I don't. I think I'm engaging my art to learn about a great many things, among them how to see and understand my upbringing as an influence in my life.

Are there any stories you've written that you feel have been misunderstood?

I've tried to write stories that expect a reader to do some work, to go back and reconsider. I hope there are many layers to explore, not all of which may be tapped in one reading. I don't want to play tricks with the reader, but I do want to create work that starts a conversation. I know that the art I love has asked, challenged, seduced me into coming back to it many times. In this light, I'd say that I feel most people are getting my stories. I do think, however, that there are folks who have taken from the story only part of what the story is trying to do and they come to put that story in a place that limits other readings. I can't say there is one particular story, but I feel that folks might gain from stories like "Kudzu," "In the Swamp," "Crusade," and "Why We Jump" if they look beyond them simply as stories about African-American life. That the characters are Black is important, but not as important as the other ideas and contexts that shape the complexities and realizations in those stories.

Why do you think your stories, which feature African-American characters, have been able to resonate so deeply with readers of all stripes?

I'm glad to know that this has happened. It's very important for me that my characters feel like real folks. The folks I know the best are Black folk, so much of my fictional world is working out of this or is working on how I look at such folk. But I very much want readers of all sorts to look at my stories and see the American experience. I think readers tap into the parts of stories that have to do with people dealing with past experience and memory and how those elements shape them today. It means much to me when readers discover a way of looking at their interior spaces through my work. Readers have talked about being drawn to the small moments, objects, gestures I observe or that function within characters' actions and memories. I am glad that these become touchstones for them on their way to other observations, reactions, and realizations in the work.

What's the next step in your writing career?
I am trying to take on several projects in fiction and nonfiction. I start out with several balls in the air and eventually I let a few drop.

What advice would you give to aspiring writers?
I'd like to say read a great deal, all over the place, not just in what you enjoy or think affirms your experience. And read much more than fiction, learn how words work all over the place. I also feel it's important to take your time with crafting the work. If you feel that writing is going to be in your life for as long as you are breathing, don't rush to send off work to be published. Take your time, take care, give your story the space to live outside of your emotional attachment to it so that you can go about seeing what it needs to live on its own.

Having said that, I also realize that more people are aiming their writing for movies and Web-based entertainment. If they are not writing for these genres, a great deal of novel and short story writing bears the signs of narratives that live in or compete with a world where most folks get their entertainment from a screen more so than turning pages in a book. I have not written for film or the Web, so I can't say my methods might work well for the writers who are developing those skills. It's difficult to expect people to write in a manner that is slower than the pace of today's dominant entertainment genres. Given this, I think the only thing that might work for any writing endeavor is to be sure that you know much about what's in the arena you plan to enter. This gets back to reading, but it really means being aware before you expect a book, online, or magazine editor, agent, webmaster, or director to believe that what you have written is the next big thing.

What have you learned about the art of storytelling that you'd like to pass on to readers and writers alike?

I'm not sure I've learned enough to say what I know is worthwhile. I'm still figuring it out, but what I will encourage is the power of sharp and precise observation. Listen. Watch. Bear witness. Engage all of these in deep ways and always wait for the moments that happen after you think you know all there is to know about what you hear, see, or experience. Look for observing and then retelling the parts of life that are not in the center of the action. I think storytelling is about how to share with others the parts of a known experience those folks have not thought about as deeply as the storyteller. The magic is in setting up a way to share it so that all gain from the sharing of story.

You have now written two collections of stories praised by the likes of Nikki Giovanni, Ann Beattie, Dave Eggers, and Edward P. Jones. Do you think you'll ever engage the novel? Is there more satisfaction in short story writing than novels? What is attractive about the art of the short story?

I'm not sure what it's like to write a novel. I have yet to put serious work into one. I've written about sixty pages on one idea that failed and I'm now trying to begin writing a new novel. It feels very challenging for me. It's not that I can't generate pages. It has more to do with how my creative instincts work. I'm more inclined to write a long short story than flow on for scores of pages. But this is something I'd like to learn how to do.

As for what's attractive about the short story, I can't say. There are two ideas from writers I admire a great deal that come to mind. Toni Morrison has said that she likes to write stories that she likes to read, which, I think, is not some sort of pompous approach to writing. I think she is setting up a challenge for herself to add to the body of writing she feels has fueled her most meaningful reading experiences. John Updike has written that being a writer is sort of like being a chicken: a chicken does not lay an egg because it wants to. In this sense, I don't think I ever wanted to write short stories as much as short stories have had to come out of me. I'm hoping a novel, a film script, essays, a few more plays (I've written a few), and poems will come out as fully formed as short stories have.